2.95

Nobody wanted to go to sleep that night. The thought that Wally might be crawling around somewhere was enough to keep all of them close to the fire. After a long period of quiet, when things were gradually settling down, Brian began to taunt them. "I think he's coming. Listen. You can hear those big old feet clumping through the brush. When Wally's mad, nothing can stop him. And you can bet he's mad right now. He's gonna come in here and start throwing bodies up into the trees. All except you, half-pint. He likes you. When he's all done with the rest, he'll take you back to camp with him."

P. J. PETERSEN lives in Redding, California. This is his second novel, following the successful *Would You Settle for Improbable?*, also available in a Dell Laurel-Leaf edition.

Nobody Else Can Walk It for You

P. J. PETERSEN

LAUREL-LEAF
BOOKS

LAUREL-LEAF BOOKS bring together under a single imprint outstanding works of fiction and nonfiction particularly suitable for young adult readers, both in and out of the classroom. Charles F. Reasoner, Professor Emeritus of Children's Literature and Reading, New York University, is consultant to this series.

Published by
Dell Publishing Co., Inc.
1 Dag Hammarskjold Plaza
New York, New York 10017

For information address Delacorte Press,
New York, New York.
Laurel-Leaf Library ® TM 766734,
Dell Publishing Co., Inc.

ISBN: 0-440-96733-3

RL: 4.7

Reprinted by arrangement with Delacorte Press
Printed in the United States of America
August 1984

10 9 8 7 6 5 4 3 2

WFH

For Marian, Karen, and Carla

Motorcycles. The first time she heard the sound, Laura Martin knew it was motorcycles. Usually when you were that far back in a wilderness area and heard a motor, you automatically looked into the sky for an airplane. But Laura knew immediately that these were motorcycles. There was no mistaking the popping and snarling of the exhausts, no matter how far away they were.

"Just what we need," Laura muttered. "Some idiots on motorcycles."

For the moment the Kingsley Y Group had Jack Pine Lake all to themselves. And they deserved it, Laura thought. If you drove a hundred miles on winding roads and then carried full packs for eight miles, you shouldn't have to share your campsite. You should be able to listen to chipmunks and frogs and wind in the trees—not motorcycles.

Laura stepped away from her tent and took a last look around. The lake, stretched out before her, was a mirror, repeating the deep green of the pine forest and the incredible blue of the sky. She turned away quickly, unable to enjoy the view. Because this was her first time to lead a backpacking trip, she had followed the manuals to the letter. She was prepared for mosquitoes, thunderstorms, sunburn, fainting spells, poison oak, even broken bones. But none of the manuals had mentioned motorcycles.

Wondering if any of the others had heard the noise, Laura looked down toward the lakeshore. Her group was splashing through a game of Keep Away. You had to be sixteen, she decided, to be able to play in that icy water. She had gone down earlier and waded a little, but the biting coldness had numbed her toes immediately. Eighteen years old and only one year out of high school, Laura watched the horseplay and felt ancient.

"Can you hear those things?" she called over her shoulder to Irene Nichols, who was banging on an old Coleman stove. Laura still felt a bit awkward about being teamed with a woman old enough to be her grandmother. The two of them were the adults of the party, the chaperones, and Laura, a paid employee of the Y, was in charge. But she couldn't help feeling like a little girl around Irene.

"What's that?" Irene asked, pushing a strand of silver-gray hair away from her face. "About the only thing I've heard was me cussing this stove. It's a good thing the kids aren't around. I might shock the little rascals."

"It's just some dumb motorcycles."

"You got better ears than I do, honey." Irene pulled a book of matches from her pants pocket, twisted a lever, and lit the stove. "There we go. Darn thing's too heavy to carry, and it's always getting plugged up, but I'm glad I brought it. There's a limit to how much cooking I want to do over a campfire. I figure campfires are good for marshmallows and wieners, and that's about it." She laughed and picked up two plastic bottles. "Are you gonna get me some water, or are you the kind of boss that just stands around and gives orders?"

"I'll get the water," Laura said.

"That's good 'cause I don't think I could make it. You just about finished me off today. An old lady like me's got no business running around out here in the hills anyway, and then this whole outfit seems to think that resting is against the law."

Laura carried the bottles down to the stream that fed into the lake. When she had first started her summer job at the Y, she had been afraid of Irene and her sharp tongue. But a small-town Y lived or died by volunteer labor, and Irene's sharp tongue always said, "Oh, I guess so," while gentler tongues were making polite excuses. Irene would complain, but she was always ready to teach a first-aid class or sell tickets at a dance. Or, Laura added, go on a five-day pack trip when the other chaperones dropped out at the last minute.

Six weeks at the Y job had taught Laura to be

flexible. When you worked with teen-agers and volun-
teers, you had to be ready for changes at any moment.
Sixteen people—twelve teen-agers and four adults—had
originally signed up for the backpacking trip, but then
the usual things happened. Somebody found a job, and
somebody else found a new boyfriend, and one girl
came down with chicken pox, and company came,
and . . .

In spite of it all, Laura had succeeded. By recruiting
Irene and reorganizing the plans and arguing down all
of her boss's objections, she had saved the trip from
being canceled. Now they were at Jack Pine Lake—
seven teen-agers and two adults. (For the time being,
Laura was placing herself in the adult category.) The
camp was set up, the weather was warm, and the
others were now swimming and playing as if they had
never made the hike. Things hadn't worked out ac-
cording to plan, of course—they never did—but they
had worked out.

When Laura returned with the water, Irene was
waiting with an empty pan. "Gotta get some coffee
going around here. Otherwise, I may not make it
through supper." She poured half a bottle of water into
the pan and moved toward the stove. "I can hear that
motorcycle now. Can't get away from it, even out here.
There's always some joker that can't follow the rules."

"It was so peaceful here," Laura moaned.

"I'd like to get hold of his machine and let the air

out of the tires. If he had to push it all the way out of here, maybe he'd think twice about bringing it back again." She set the pan on the stove and adjusted the flame.

"Maybe they won't come this far."

"They better not," Irene said. "They come around here, I'll send 'em packing."

"You would, too. How's Beverly doing? She said her foot was bothering her."

"Don't worry about that one. She didn't even have a blister. All she's got is a bad case of the pretties—too pretty to do any work. Doesn't want to get her little hands dirty. As soon as camp was all set up, she was fine. She wasn't going to miss swimming—not with the bathing suit she had."

Laura grinned. "Well, it didn't take up much space in her pack."

"That's for sure. That thing'd fit in a matchbox with room to spare. She might as well wear a couple of Band-Aids and forget it."

"I'm glad she's feeling better anyway," Laura said.

"I wouldn't worry about her. Every group has to have a stinker, and she's it for this crowd."

"She really isn't so bad," Laura said. "She's been having a tough time at home. Her parents are divorced, and her mother is about to remarry—"

"That psychology business is all right for you, I guess. Me, I don't care why they do it. If they're stinkers, they're stinkers." She repositioned her pan with a pair of insulated pliers.

"I guess it's about time to start a fire," Laura said, changing the subject.

"Yeah, it is. If they're gonna cook hot dogs, they better get the fire going so it can burn down a ways. We could go ahead and start it easy enough, but these greenhorns better do some of the work just so they don't start thinking they're on vacation."

"I'll go down and get some of them," Laura said.

"Don't bother. Just plug your ears." Irene stood up, placed two fingers in her mouth, and produced a piercing whistle that would have served a factory.

"Wow," Laura said.

"That oughta get their attention." Irene whistled once more, then yelled, "We need two of you for fire crew."

Laura watched the Gray twins dash out of the water and grab their shoes. The Grays were a strange pair— the Odd Couple, the kids at the Y called them. Fraternal twins, they were as unlike as two people could be. One was tall and thin and red-haired; the other was shorter, round-faced, and blond. What made the contrast striking was that the tall one was Donna and the short one, John. Both twins were sensitive about their respective sizes, each envying the other's stature.

The two of them raced up the hill toward the camp, pushing and shoving as they ran. "You'd better let me light the fire, klutzo," Donna shouted. "You know your mommy doesn't let you play with matches."

"Your mommy *wants* you to play with matches," John shouted back. "When you were little, she would always send you out to play with a book of matches and a can of gasoline."

"Get some dead twigs for kindling," Laura told them. The twins, still squabbling, immediately began scouring the brush beyond the clearing. They were good kids, Laura thought, even if they got a little tiresome with their game of low blows. The insults never seemed to bother them, though, and Laura couldn't remember ever seeing them really angry at each other. She couldn't remember a tender word between them either.

Moving downhill toward the lake, Laura saw that the Keep Away game was over. Beverly was sunbathing, and somebody else was wrapped in a towel. Chris and Stephanie were standing in knee-deep water, holding hands as they stared at each other. Stephanie, with her bright eyes, had a smile that would melt granite. It was no wonder that Chris Taylor could scarcely tie his shoes when she was around. Laura wondered briefly if that little romance was going to be a problem before the trip was over.

"Hey, Laura," Louie Shaw yelled. She watched him come up the path toward her, wearing the bright flowered shirt he always put on as soon as he came out of the water. Louie was painfully conscious of his round

basketball stomach, which made people think of Santa
Claus. He had his hands cupped in front of him, and
he kept peering into them. "Look at this, Laura."

"If it has a lot of legs, I don't want it near me,"
Laura said.

"It's nothing like that. It's really amazing, though."

Laura sensed a trick. Louie had that look on his face.
"If it's something nasty and dead, I don't even want to
see it."

"No, it's nothing like that." As Louie came closer to
her, he bent over and peered more intently into his
hands. "Here. Take a look for yourself."

When Laura, in spite of her better judgment, leaned
forward to look, Louie suddenly raised his hands and
threw water into her face. "Gotcha!" he yelled.

"You rat," Laura shouted and made a halfhearted
grab at him as he dashed back toward the water.

"See," he called back. "I told you it wasn't dead or
dirty or anything."

Hearing a roar high above her, Laura turned away
from Louie, toward the mountain that loomed above
them. A lone motorcycle had stopped at the overlook.
As she watched, a second cycle appeared, and then a
third. For a moment the three riders' helmets stood
in a row. Then the motors roared, and the cycles moved
down the switchbacked trail toward the lake.

"That's three too many," Laura muttered, "but at
least there isn't a whole gang of them." She started
back toward the campsite. The fire was burning by

then, and black smoke was rising from the pitchy pine branches.

"Laura! Laura!" Amy Falkenberry was shouting as she ran uphill. There was no mistaking that voice—low-pitched and full of authority. John Gray always said that Amy was studying to become a dictator. "Do you see them?"

"They're a little hard to miss," Laura said as Amy stopped beside her.

Amy's lips were tight, almost disappearing. She was a tiny girl, short and thin, but her voice should have belonged to a two hundred pounder. "That's against the law. This is a wilderness area, and all motorcycles are forbidden. There's a big sign back there at the start of the trail."

"I remember."

"They're banned for good reason, too. They scare the animals, they damage the trails and cause erosion, and they annoy people." She looked up at Laura as if she expected an argument.

"They annoy me—that's for sure," Laura said.

"Those people ought to be arrested."

"Suits me. Have you seen any cops around?" Amy glared at her. "Come on, Amy, I hate the noisy things, too, but there's nothing we can do about it."

Amy snorted. "We'll see. If they don't get out of here, I'm going to take down their license plates and report them when we get back." She turned back toward the lake.

Laura picked up a handful of sticks and carried them into camp. Irene looked up from the stove and said, "Must be our lucky day."

Laura tossed her wood onto the pile. "Those things sure make a racket, don't they?"

"They got no business in here with those machines, and I got a good mind to tell 'em so." Laura laughed quietly but said nothing. "I mean it. People like that don't have the brains God gave a goose."

Laura moved beside the fire and watched the meadow where the riders would appear. Irene, bent over the stove again, mumbled something that Laura couldn't hear.

The first of the bikers emerged from the trees and shot out onto the flat. He leaned backward suddenly, and the front wheel of the cycle rose from the ground. He moved across the meadow in that position. When the front wheel dropped, he jammed his foot into the ground and spun the cycle in a half circle, spraying dirt and rocks into the air.

A second cycle came onto the meadow, and a third, while the first rider sat and adjusted the straps on his canvas knapsack. The cycles were not the stripped-down trail bikes that you occasionally saw in the mountains. They were lightweight street cycles with headlights and fenders. And license plates, Laura noted. That would make Amy happy. Above the license plates, dusty bedrolls were lashed to the backs of the seats.

Laura stood and watched, wondering whether she

should walk down to the newcomers. Was it better to be friendly or to ignore them? She wished they would take off their helmets, which made them look like beings from outer space. Before Laura could make a decision, Irene was marching up to the first cyclist, her gray hair bouncing with each step. "All right, buddy boy," she shouted. "You can turn that thing around and head right on out of here."

The rider unsnapped his chin strap, lifted off his helmet, and ran his fingers through his dark, matted hair. Looking at him from that distance, Laura judged him to be about her age, perhaps a year younger. He grinned at Irene as he reached down and switched off his motor. The other riders did the same. The sudden silence was almost as jarring as the engines had been.

The cyclist looked at Irene for a minute, as if he could not decide if he should laugh. "Hey, lady, what's the problem?"

"You're the problem," Irene said. "You got no business in a wilderness area on a motorcycle. You just turn around and head on out of here."

Looking toward the lake, the cyclist reached inside his denim jacket and brought out a package of cigarettes. He removed a cigarette, tapped it several times on his thumbnail, and then reached into a pocket for a match. He struck the match on his belt buckle and stared at the flame for a few seconds before using it. During the whole process he did not once look at Irene. He inhaled slowly, blew out the smoke in a long, thin line, and said, "Is this a wilderness area, lady? It just looks like more of the same to me."

"You passed a big sign right at the trailhead. If you get caught in here with a motorcycle, it'll be confiscated."

"Well, lady, I tell ya. We better not let that happen, right?"

"You can just turn yourself around right now and get on out of here," Irene said. "There are plenty of places for you to take those things where it's legal."

"Yeah, lady, but we're kind of hot. You know what I mean? We been riding a long ways, and we're hot. And there's a lake right here, and it looks real nice and cool. So I think me and my friends here, we're gonna have a swim. Then we'll see what we feel like. Maybe we'll go, and maybe we'll stay. You know what I mean?"

"You're just asking for trouble," Irene said. "If I were you, I'd ride on out of here right now."

"Yeah, well, you're not me. If you was me, you'd know how hot I am. Not asking for trouble, lady. It wasn't me that came out yelling at people, telling them what to do. I just fly easy, and I let other people do the same. And if they're smart, that's what they do. Right now I'm gonna go swimming." He dropped his cigarette on the ground, mashed it with his boot, and then tramped down on the starter. The engine caught and roared. Then the other two started their cycles, and the air was filled with sound and blue smoke. The black-haired cyclist replaced his helmet and veered around Irene.

As the cyclists followed the trail toward the Y group's tents, Laura realized that she was still standing in the same spot. She wished she had joined Irene, maybe held the old woman back a little. Or at least stopped her when there wasn't any point in continuing. But the time for action was gone, and Laura felt helpless and stupid for having done nothing. She lifted her hand in an impersonal wave as the cycles skirted the edge of the camp, then disappeared over the rise.

A few minutes later the noise of the engines stopped, and Laura knew that the riders were at the campsite closest to the water's edge. Earlier that afternoon she had considered that site before deciding that the extra shade where they were was more important than being near the water.

Irene stalked back to her stove. "That's a real outfit for you," she said to Laura. "I don't mind having people around when I camp, but those three don't count as people." She began to rummage in her knapsack, pulling out packages and throwing them back. "I'd better get started cooking, I guess. I don't see anybody else trying to beat me out of my job."

"I'll be happy to do whatever—"

Irene looked at Laura and then grinned. "Come on, honey. Let an old lady fuss a little, will you? I'm tired, and I'm mad, and fussing's one of the few pleasures I got left. If I want you to do something, I'll tell you. I don't know if you noticed, but I ain't bashful." She held up a package of dried apples. "I knew these things were down there somewhere. Tell you what. Why don't you send me a helper or two? And maybe you better head down by the lake and make sure those jokers aren't skinny-dipping."

"And what if they are?" Laura asked, laughing as she spoke.

"Then you tell the little girls to hide their eyes, I guess. I'll leave it up to you. You're the boss lady."

By the time Laura reached the lake, the three riders were already in the water. They were swimming close to their campsite, a good hundred yards from where Laura's group was now quietly wading and stealing glances at the newcomers. The bikers *had* kept their jeans on, Laura noted thankfully. "Who's going to help Irene?" she asked.

"Chris and I will," Stephanie said, taking Chris's hand. "I'm starting to turn blue anyway."

"Sure. I'm a great cook," Chris said. They waded to shore and slipped on their sandals.

Laura smiled as they came past her. She wondered what Chris would do if Stephanie suggested that they jump off a cliff. Probably smile, grab her hand, and jump, she decided.

Once Stephanie and Chris were out of the water, the others began to move toward the shoreline. "Hey,

Laura," Louie yelled, "this is really interesting." He moved toward her with his hands cupped in front of him.

"Get out of here," Laura said. Louie laughed and showed her his empty hands. He came out of the water quickly and pulled on his flowered shirt.

Laura kept watching the bikers out of the corner of her eye. They were some distance from the shore, with only their heads bobbing above water. She didn't know whether they were standing on the bottom or swimming. As she watched her own group come out of the water, she realized that she hadn't seen Beverly. "Where's Bev anyway?"

"She was here sunbathing a few minutes ago," Donna Gray said. "Old Superklutz here just about fell on his nose when he went past her."

"But where is she now?"

"I don't know," Donna said. "John should, though. He's the official bikini inspector for the camp, and he takes his job very seriously."

"I don't know where she went," John said to Laura, then turned back to his sister. "You better watch out, or I'll tell them about the time you wore a topless bathing suit."

"I did nothing of the kind," Donna said, not laughing.

"There Donna was, walking down the beach, topless. And the first person she saw was a policeman. You

know what he said? He said, 'Hello, sir.' " John picked
up his towel and went dashing up the hill.

"I don't blame you," Donna called after him. "I'd
run off, too, if I told a joke as old as that." She pulled
on her shoes and followed after him.

Amy Falkenberry, who always seemed a little uneasy
around the Gray twins, came up close to Laura. "I'm
not sure, but I think Bev may have gone up where
those new guys are."

"Don't tell me," Laura said.

"Right after those guys went into the water, she got
up and went somewhere. And she's not really the kind
to go off for a nature hike, especially in her bathing
suit."

"She may be up at our camp," Laura said. "I don't see
her anywhere."

"I don't know why she came in the first place," Amy
went on. "She's done nothing but complain all day. If
she didn't want to hike, she shouldn't have signed up
for a backpack trip."

"Give her a chance," Laura said. "This may be a bad
day for her."

"After all," Amy continued, "if you're going to hike,
you're going to get hot and tired. That's just part of it."

"I hope you two aren't talking about me over there,"
Louie shouted.

"We really aren't," Laura said. "But if you can give
us some good juicy gossip about yourself, we can start."

"Well," Louie said, coming toward them, "I hate to

tell on her, but Amy's been getting awfully fresh with me. I keep telling her I'm not that kind of person, but she won't take no for an answer."

"Very funny," Amy said.

"Don't feel bad," Louie said, starting up the hill. "You're not the first girl to find me irresistible."

Amy turned her back to him. "You're sick. You really are."

Laura walked down to the water's edge and retrieved a tube of suntan lotion that somebody had left behind. She glanced toward the other campsite and saw the bikers still in the water. However, instead of listlessly floating, they were shouting and splashing and ducking each other. Laura suspected the reason for the change even before she caught sight of the orange bathing suit.

"Do you see that?" Amy said. "It was too cold for her to swim before. And now look at her."

Laura stooped over and rinsed off her hands. She wanted to rush up the beach and tell that brainless Beverly to get back to her own group. She glanced that way again and saw that they were playing King of the Mountain on a protruding log.

As Laura turned away, Amy asked, "Aren't you going to do something?"

"Yeah, I am. I'm going to walk up the hill and see how dinner's coming."

"I mean about Beverly. I don't think she ought to be over there with those creeps."

"I don't either," Laura said, "but it won't be for long. Let's go check the food."

As they walked up the hill, Laura purposely did not look back at the other campsite. There was little need. Amy provided a complete description. "Now she's up on one guy's shoulders. He's carrying her around that way. Sometimes I can't believe her. She's just asking for trouble. She really is."

"I wouldn't worry about it," Laura said. But soon after reaching camp, she asked Chris to go tell Beverly that dinner was ready. "She's up by the other campsite," she added, as if it were an afterthought.

As she watched Chris squeeze Stephanie's hand and trot off along the trail, Laura realized that she had sent the largest male in her group.

II

As the mountains began to dissolve into the oncoming darkness, Laura stood back from the campfire and enjoyed a moment of self-satisfaction. The evening meal had gone by without a hitch. All the things that needed to be done before dark had been done. So now everyone was full, the wet bathing suits were hanging from a limb, the dishes were scrubbed, and the marshmallows were ready.

The bikers were still at the lake, of course, but at least they had stayed to themselves since Beverly came back for dinner.

Laura watched the others push close to the fire. Earlier there had been talk of a moonlight swim, but nobody seemed likely to mention it again.

Irene, metal coffee cup in hand, came over to where Laura was standing. "Well, I think this tribe'll sleep tonight. You got a surefire method going. Get 'em up at the crack of dawn, run their tails off all day, and then they're too tired for monkey business at night."

"I don't know about them," Laura said, "but I'm ready for bed right now."

"You better have some of this coffee. You got a long way left to go. It's too bad you couldn't talk one of the fathers into coming along. We could have acted helpless and put him on night patrol."

"Melanie Vincent's father was going to come, but then she came down with chicken pox."

"It's just as well," Irene said. "He'd be trying to run the whole show, and you wouldn't get a chance to earn your money."

"I'd better start earning my money right now," Laura said. "Everybody's just hanging around."

Laura floated through the next half hour. She had been leading choirs since she started high school. Give her a group of people around a campfire, and she was immediately in control. She knew how to encourage the timid singers, how to draw out the reluctant ones. Once she got them to quit thinking about themselves, the rest was easy.

This group turned out to be singers—a few hangers-back at first, but you had to expect that from high schoolers. Once she had them started, it was just a matter of choosing the right song and stopping it soon enough.

When they broke for marshmallows, Laura moved back away from the fire. She had no interest in a charred marshmallow. All she wanted was a few breaths of the crisp night air. At that elevation the temperature had started down with the sun, and now the air had a bite to it that was refreshing and soothing—for a minute anyway.

As Laura leaned against a tree and watched the Gray twins try to force each other's marshmallows into the flames, she heard a rustling in the darkness. Then there was the flare of a match and the glow of a cigarette a few feet beyond her, just out of the light of the camp-fire.

"What are you doing here?" Laura said, speaking before she had full control of her voice.

"Not much. Just listening to the singing. You guys are good. What are you, some kind of choir or something?"

In spite of her misgivings, Laura was pleased at the compliment. "No. Not a choir. Just a Y group. They *are* good singers, though."

The cigarette glowed, then moved closer. Laura could barely make out the face, but she could see that he was the one who had talked to Irene that afternoon. "I'm Brian," he said.

Laura took a step back toward the campfire. "Hello, Brian. I'm Laura."

"You're Laura?" He sounded doubtful.

"That's me."

"You're the one in charge?"

"That's me again."

"Hey, that's wild. When Beverly said that the old lady that was screaming at us wasn't even in charge, that it was somebody named Laura, I didn't figure it would be somebody like you."

"Well," Laura said, "I'd better get the singing going again. Otherwise, we'll be out of marshmallows."

"Hey, Laura," Brian said as she started away, "you think it'd be okay if we joined you? We're pretty good singers. Me and Wally anyway. Myron's not so hot."

The mention of the names caused Laura to look into the darkness beyond Brian. She could make out the shapes of the other two, hanging back from the light. "I don't know," Laura said. "This is kind of a special thing. We're all part of a group back home." She could feel herself floundering. "Part of the reason we go on a trip like this is to build up a sense of togetherness. It sort of defeats the purpose if we bring in outsiders. It's nothing against you fellows or anything."

Laura sensed, rather than heard, his laughter. "Yeah, well, what's it gonna hurt, huh, Laura? We're camping right over there. What's it gonna hurt if we come over here and sing songs with you guys? It'd be kind of dumb for the three of us to sit over there and sing songs. You know what I mean? I mean, look, three guys like us, we can't sit around and sing. Besides, all we hear over at our camp is you guys over here having fun."

Laura found herself looking over her shoulder for Irene. But that was silly. This was her decision and hers alone.

Brian moved closer to her, close enough for her to see his face clearly. It was an appealing face, she thought, an attractive face, even with the sneering upper lip that seemed to be natural to him. The eyes, though, were dark and distant. "What do you say, Laura? We're not gonna cause any trouble. We just want to sit down and sing with you. No problems. No trouble. What's it gonna hurt?"

"All right," Laura said. "Come on. I'll introduce you to the group." As she moved toward the fire, she was immediately aware of the silence. She realized the whole group had been watching her. "Hey, gang," she said as brightly as she could, "I have some more recruits. This is Brian." Brian looked across the fire at the others and gave his head a toss. "You'll have to introduce your friends."

"Yeah, well, this is Wally," Brian said. Wally towered over the others. He had the shoulders of a football player, but his enormous chest gave way to an even more enormous stomach that hung out over his belt. He had a short reddish blond beard and long, stringy hair that was darker than the beard. He swaggered over to the fire, casually looking over the group. "And back there is Myron." Myron stayed at the edge of the circle, leaning against a tree. He smiled and looked down at his feet. He seemed younger than the others, Laura thought, but that might have been because of his shyness. He was lean, with long arms and legs that made him appear more awkward than he probably was.

"Everybody gather around," Laura called, once more the choir director. "Let's start with 'Kumbayah.' "

It took two or three verses for the group to relax and really to sing. Once they were started, Brian joined enthusiastically. Wally's voice, loud and deep, was vigorous from the beginning, sometimes on key, sometimes not. He was serious while he sang, as if concentrating on each note. Myron stayed back from the rest. His lips moved, but Laura could not tell if he was actually singing. She sidled toward him and motioned for him to join the circle. He grinned at her, then shook his head and looked down at his feet.

"Hey, Myron," Brian yelled when the song was finished, "get your ugly self over here."

"I'm okay," Myron said.

"Are you coming, or are we gonna have to drag you over here?"

Myron looked at his feet. "He's all right," Laura said quickly. "Do you all know 'Lonesome Valley'?"

"Never heard of it," John said.

"It's really easy. It goes, 'You got to walk that lonesome valley. You got to walk it by yourself. Nobody else can walk it for you. You got to walk it by yourself.' "

"That's the backpacker's theme song," Louie shouted.

"Let's give it a try," Laura said.

Like Myron, Irene stayed outside the circle, occasionally sipping from her metal cup. Laura did not look in that direction, but she knew that Irene would be grumbling and frowning. But Laura was the one in charge, and she was rather pleased that the apparent problem had been solved so easily.

After a half hour they stopped for another round of marshmallows. Brian and Beverly moved back away from the campfire while Brian smoked a cigarette. Somebody handed Wally a stick, and he grinned as he stood and toasted his marshmallow. Laura carried a marshmallow and stick to Myron, but he shook his head. "That's okay."

"Hey, rubbergut," Donna shouted at her brother, "leave some for the rest of us."

"That did it," John shouted back. "One look at your face, and I've lost my appetite."

Stephanie and Chris fed each other marshmallows while Louie set his on fire and then stood at attention and shouted, "The Statue of Liberty."

Laura breathed deeply and smiled at the return of normality. She stole a quick look at Irene, who was sitting on a log and staring into her cup. "All right," Laura called. "A few more songs before we quit. Do you know 'Jacob's Ladder'?"

The campfire ended with a group of spirituals, a botched-up ghost story that Louie insisted on telling, and finally Laura's prayer of thanks for the day. When the prayer was finished, Laura was all business. "All right now. I want everybody in the sack in fifteen minutes. We have a long way to go tomorrow, and I don't want anybody dogging it. Brian, Myron, Wally

—thanks for joining us. The extra voices made quite a difference. If any of you people have blisters, be sure that you have Irene check them. I don't want anybody going lame on us."

Laura moved away from the fire, back to where Irene was sitting. "I don't know what you're thinking about," Irene muttered to her. "It was bad enough having those jokers around here. I don't know why you had to bring 'em right in. It's like inviting the fox into the henhouse."

"Oh," Laura said easily, "it didn't hurt anything."

"Mrs. Nichols," Amy Falkenberry called, "could you come and look at this place on my heel?"

"Is your leg broken?" Irene shouted back. "Did you sprain your ankle?"

"No, I just have this place on my heel."

"Then you bring it over here. I don't make house calls if I can help it."

Laura turned back to the campfire. Chris and Stephanie were standing by the fire, holding hands and looking into each other's eyes. Laura first groaned, then laughed at herself for being that way. Then she saw Beverly and Brian standing back in the shadows.

"All right, Chris and Stephanie," Laura called. "It's time to get the camp buttoned down for the night. Say your good nights and go." As she spoke, she kept her eye on Beverly and Brian.

Chris and Stephanie walked to the shadows, stopped

beside Stephanie's tent, and exchanged a quick kiss. Then Chris came back across to the tent that he and John Gray were sharing.

Beverly moved away from Brian, and Laura felt herself beginning to smile. She had handled things properly, she thought, by not speaking directly to Beverly. As she started back to where Irene was working on Amy's foot, she felt like skipping. Then she heard her name called.

"Yes, Bev?"

Beverly came toward her, somehow managing—even in hiking boots—to maintain her customary strut. "Laura," she said, "I'll be back in a few minutes. Brian and I are going for a walk."

Laura held herself back from the reply she wanted to make. She waited until she could speak calmly and quietly. "Not tonight, Bev. It's bedtime for all of us."

"Oh, come on," Beverly said. "I won't be gone very long. I never go to bed at this time of night when I'm home."

"I'm sorry," Laura said, trying for total finality in her voice.

"It isn't like I've never been out on a date," Beverly said. "I was going steady when I was twelve. We're just going for a walk."

"I'm sorry, Bev. It's time to call it a night."

"I don't see what gives you the right . . ." Beverly began.

"I'm not going to argue with you," Laura cut in.

Beverly's head dropped down, and Laura felt herself relax. "It's not fair," Beverly said.

"Probably not," Laura said. "But that's the way it is." As she looked past Beverly's shoulder, she saw Brian move toward them. "Now be a good sport, take thirty seconds to say good night, and then go to your tent."

"Hey, what's the problem?" Brian asked, smiling as he spoke.

"It's bedtime here, Brian," Laura said. "We enjoyed having you join us."

Beverly turned toward him. "She says I can't go for a walk."

Brian laughed. "Hey, Laura, how old are you?"

"What difference does that make?"

"Well, you look pretty young to be Bev's mommy."

"Bev," Laura said, struggling to keep her voice pleasant, "your thirty seconds have already started."

"I don't know about you, kid," Brian said to Beverly. "You look pretty big to need a baby-sitter."

"The thirty seconds are still going," Laura said.

"Oh, come here," Beverly said, taking Brian's hand and leading him away from the fire. The two of them stood, arms around each other, and whispered.

Laura spent a minute shoving the smoldering ends of the logs onto the middle of the fire. Irene was suddenly beside her. "Listen," Irene muttered, "we're going to get that joker out of this camp if I have to take a stick after him."

"He's going," Laura said. "I told them they could have thirty seconds."

"And they've had five minutes. I knew that girl was going to be a pill right from the first."

"It's all right," Laura said. "I'll send him off in just a minute."

"We'll see, I guess."

Laura shoved a stick into the middle of the orange coals and turned away. "All right, Bev. I know it's too dark to see your watch, but you know that your time is up."

"Okay," Beverly said, not moving.

Laura waited long enough to count a slow ten and then moved toward them. "All right. Bedtime."

"You're hard to believe," Brian said. "I mean, you got nothing better to do with your time than bother us."

"Right now, Beverly," Laura said.

Beverly said something that Laura did not catch and started to step away. "Not so fast," Brian said. He caught her hand and pulled her toward him. He wrapped his arms around her and kissed her fiercely, bending her backward as he did so. When he released her, she tripped and almost fell. "You get your kicks out of watching, Laura?" He laughed and walked away into the darkness. When he had gone a few steps, he stopped and lit a cigarette and laughed again. His laughter seemed to penetrate the entire camp.

"Well," Laura said, walking back to Irene, "he's gone anyway."

"For now," Irene said.

"You think he'll be back?"

"I wouldn't bet against it. I'll tell you what. You let everything get real quiet, and you keep your eye on little Beverly's tent."

"Oh, I don't think Beverly—" Laura stopped herself. "Actually, you're probably right. She's okay on her own, but when she gets around boys, it's another story."

"You go get your things laid out," Irene said. "I'll sit here and keep my eyes open. When you come back, I'll go get some sleep."

Laura looked into the fire. "I guess I did wrong tonight. I thought it would be better to be friendly than get them mad."

"Who knows, honey? Let's take it from here. With clowns like those, I'm not sure there *is* a right way."

A half hour later the fire had burned down to a pile of coals, but Laura made no move to add wood. The night was cool, but she was comfortable in her down-filled jacket. Besides, she did not want to advertise her presence. If there was going to be a problem with Beverly, Laura wanted it to come as soon as possible.

She had been up since dawn, and she didn't know how much longer she could sit before drifting off.

At the other campsite a huge fire was burning. Laura couldn't see it from where she sat, but she could see its light penetrating the blackness. One of the boys was swimming. She could hear the splashing and the shouts. Laura decided it must be Wally.

She kept moving her head around, trying to keep herself alert. Whenever her eyelids began to slip together, she took a number of deep breaths and flexed her hands and feet. It was hard to believe that you could be so tired that you could fall asleep sitting on a log.

When she first saw the movement at Beverly's tent, Laura wasn't sure what it had been. She waited and watched, her eyes open now. A crouching figure was moving slowly away from the tent. Laura waited until the figure was some distance from the tent before she turned on her flashlight.

Beverly stood there motionless for a moment, then slowly turned toward the light, protecting her eyes with her open hand. Laura lowered the beam of light so that it rested on Beverly's feet.

"I had to go to the bathroom," Beverly said.

"Where's your flashlight?"

"Right here. I didn't want to wake anybody."

"You're turned around. The area we set up for you girls is down that way."

Beverly changed direction and walked away from Laura. "It all kind of looks the same in the dark."

Laura waited by the fire until Beverly returned. "Bev, over here."

"What's the matter?"

"I want you to promise me that you'll stay in your tent until morning."

Beverly looked down at her flashlight. "I was just . . ."

"Come on, Bev. That's not asking much."

"I was just going to the bathroom. Gosh, I don't see why you have to go thinking . . ."

"Take your choice. Either you promise me to stay in your tent, or you can share a tent with me. Irene can move in with Amy."

"I don't know why you have to go picking on me. I wasn't doing anything. I just had to go to the bathroom." She began to sniffle. "Gosh, I can't even go to the bathroom without you getting all mad at me."

"Save it," Laura said. "You can tell me about it while we bunk together."

"It's none of your business anyway. What do you care? As soon as I get home from this stupid trip, I can go out with anybody I want to and stay out as long as I want."

"I'm not going to argue with you. Just grab your sleeping bag and come on. You and I are going to be roommates."

"Gosh, I don't see . . ."

—"You don't have to see. Just get your sleeping bag."

Beverly took one step toward her tent, then stopped. "Oh, all right, if it'll make you happy. I promise I won't come out of my tent again tonight. But I don't see why you have to be so . . ."

"That's all I wanted to hear," Laura said. "Now go to bed. If we're going to have a debate, we'll have it when I'm not so tired. Good night."

Once Beverly had crawled inside her tent, Laura snapped off the flashlight and returned to the log. Slowly her night vision returned to her. As the minutes passed, she could make out the trees and the clumps of brush that stood beyond the clearing. If nothing else, the skirmish with Beverly had served to get Laura's blood flowing. She was still tired, but she could control her eyes.

After a time she got up and walked across the circle. The light from the other fire no longer glowed against the trees, and Laura wondered if the boys over there had gone to sleep. She decided to walk to the top of the rise and take a look. If they were asleep, then she could get some rest, too.

The sounds of a summer night echoed across the lake. A night bird called, and another answered. The frogs continued their serenade. Laura crept along the trail, preferring to grope through the moonlight rather than use her flashlight.

As she reached the top of the rise, she could see the

other campfire. Nothing seemed to be moving around it. She felt her body relax, and she stood for a moment, letting the breeze toss her hair.

Just down the trail a match scraped and a flame appeared. Laura forced herself to stand still as the flame went to a cigarette and then disappeared, replaced by the glowing coal. Standing there, Laura was acutely conscious of the sulfur odor of the match and then the smell of cigarette smoke.

She turned and started back toward her camp, moving an inch at a time. Brian was only twenty feet away, but he hadn't heard or seen her. As she sidestepped back, she watched the glow of the cigarette brighten and then fade.

There was no special noise, no snapped twig or missed step. But Brian suddenly said, "Bev?" and flipped on his light.

Laura turned on her own light immediately. "Bev's asleep," she said evenly. "She won't be coming out here."

Brian snapped off his flashlight. The cigarette glowed once more. "Yeah, well, you're the real life of the party, you know that?"

Laura turned off her light as well. "I'd really appreciate it if you'd go back to your camp and get some sleep so that I can do the same."

"Nobody's keeping you up."

"I noticed."

"How old are you, Laura?" Brian asked, his voice turning playful.

"What difference does it make?"

"I was thinking, see? I was thinking about why you'd be giving us a hard time. I mean, what's it to you what Beverly and I do? Maybe you're a little jealous. You ever think that?"

"Oh, sure," Laura said sarcastically.

"Maybe you don't want anybody else to have any fun if you can't have any. Maybe you want to be the one to go for a walk. Maybe you don't want to be left out."

Laura began to back up. There was a threat in Brian's voice that had little to do with the words he was saying. "Come on," she said. "I get paid to do a job, and I'm just trying to earn my money. Now why don't you help me out by going back to your camp and leaving us alone?"

"Yeah, well, you really don't want me to do that, Laura. You say it, but you don't really mean it."

"Yes, I *do*," Laura said. "I'm tired of this. And I'm just plain tired. You can save your games for somebody else. I've had enough of them."

Brian dropped his cigarette and ground it out with his boot. "Come here, Laura."

"Get out of here," she said, fighting to keep her voice steady. She began to move back toward the camp again. "We don't want anything to do with you."

"I don't like this, Laura. I don't like people messing with me. I'm being nice to you, but you can't be half-way nice back. All you can do is be smart and give orders like you're my boss or something. I don't like that, Laura. That might work with your Y-group turkeys, but not with me. Nobody messes with me, Laura. You better learn that quick, or you'll be sorry."

Laura continued to edge backward. "Look," she said as calmly as she could, "I'm tired. I've been up since four o'clock this morning, and I don't feel like playing games. If I hurt your feelings, I'm sorry."

"Don't give me that. Hurt my feelings? Listen, you scraggy witch, you couldn't hurt my feelings. You're asking for it. I'm telling you. You're just asking for it." He began to move toward her.

As Laura moved backward, she realized that her hand was in her jacket pocket, clutching her knife. "I don't want any problems with you," she said softly. "You and your friends came over to join us, and I let you. Now that the campfire is over, we'll leave you alone, and we'd like to be left alone."

"Well, see, Laura, it's not that easy. You think you can treat me this way and then just forget it? I don't have to take that from people like you. You're nothing to me. All your fancy acting and your big shot Y-group stuff—that's nothing to me."

"I'm tired," Laura said. "I'm going back to camp now. I would really appreciate it—it would be a real favor if you could let us get some sleep."

Brian laughed softly. "That's better. You ought to talk about favors. See, that's all you can do. You can't boss me around. You can't tell me what to do. If I feel like it, I can take apart your whole camp. I can take you apart, and nobody can stop me. I might not do it, Laura. But you better remember that I can. I can do it anytime I feel like it. So you better be nice to me. You want something from me, you say 'please.' And you say it like you mean it."

Laura took the knife from her pocket and slowly pried open the blade. "You're right, Brian. I'm sorry if I was insulting."

He laughed again. "That's better. See? You don't have to be snotty. You want something, you tell me. But you be real sure that you say 'please.' And you ask—you don't give me orders."

Laura glanced over her shoulder at the dark campsite behind her. She wondered if anybody was still awake. "All right," she said. "I'll remember that."

"You do that," he said seriously. "You remember it. Because there's just you and us out here, and you better not forget it. I'm not hard to get along with, see, but I don't want anybody messing with me."

"Brian," Laura said, her voice just above a whisper, "I'm exhausted. I would like to go back to my tent and get some sleep." She paused for a minute and clenched her teeth. "Could I please do that?"

Brian snickered. "Okay. You do that. See? I'm easy to get along with. You can go ahead and go."

"Thank you, Brian," she whispered. "Good night."

He laughed and lit another cigarette. Laura turned and walked quickly back to the camp. As soon as she passed the first tent, which happened to be Louie's, she crouched down and waited. Everything was quiet. She scanned the rise for the glowing cigarette but could see nothing.

After a few minutes of waiting, she made her way to the tent she was sharing with Irene. She listened outside first, then eased open the flap. The tent was empty. Laura stood up and waited, searching the darkness for any kind of movement. "Irene?" she whispered. "Irene?"

A beam of light appeared at the edge of the clearing. "I'm right over here." Irene came tramping over to the tent.

"That Brian," Laura began, "he was—"

Irene put her arm around Laura's shoulder. "I know, honey. I heard you talking and went up there. I was just behind you. If he had come close to you, I would have mashed his head like a watermelon."

Laura felt her throat begin to tighten. "I was so scared." She tried to blink back her tears.

"You handled it just right. Don't go falling apart now. That guy's a real squirrel, but you got him to leave. I waited until he went on back to his camp."

"What are we going to do?" Laura asked.

"You're doing fine," Irene said. "You tell me."

"Irene," Laura pleaded, "I'm so tired."

"Then you better get some sleep. If it was me, I think I'd get my sleeping bag and toss it right in front of Beverly's tent. That way I could get some sleep without worrying. It's not too cold tonight, and there aren't any mosquitoes. You don't need the tent."

"Good," Laura said. "That's what I'll do."

"I think we're all through for tonight," Irene said. "But if you hear anything—anything at all—you let out a whoop. I'll be there in a jiffy. And whatever happens, don't you go wandering off into the brush again."

Laura carried her sleeping bag over and arranged it directly in front of Beverly's tent. Before she lay down, she zipped open the tent flap far enough to make certain that both girls were inside. As she listened to the rhythmic breathing, Laura was both relieved and a little resentful. She had to fight off the urge to wake Beverly, who had no right to be sleeping so peacefully.

Laura lay in her sleeping bag for some time. As tired as she was, sleep did not come easily. She kept thinking of Brian and the warnings and anger that lay beneath his talk. She listened to the night sounds around her, trying to hear anything unusual. Finally she reached into the pocket of her jacket, which was serving as her pillow. She removed her knife and placed it beneath the jacket, where she could grab it in a hurry.

III

Usually on the first night of a camping trip, Laura slept fitfully, turning from side to side in the confining sleeping bag. That night, however, she scarcely moved. She awoke in the morning only after being nudged several times. Irene, kneeling beside her, whispered, "It's seven o'clock. You might as well haul your bag back to our tent. That way you don't have to explain anything."

Laura nodded and dragged herself from the bag. Moving quickly once she was out in the cold morning air, she pulled on her socks and stiff boots, then slipped into the jacket that had been her pillow. When her knife fell to the ground, she shivered as she grabbed it and stuffed it into her pocket. Then she carried her sleeping bag quickly to her tent.

"I got some water heating," Irene said. "You want me to make you some hot cocoa?"

"That would be great," Laura said, warming her hands by the stove. A chipmunk appeared in the far side of the clearing, stood on its hind feet and chattered, then dashed behind a tree. Laura yawned and stretched as the animal scampered into the open and then behind another tree. All the events of the night before seemed distant and a little silly.

Irene poured boiling water over the powder in Laura's tin cup, then dropped a marshmallow into the mixture. "That's for being a good girl. I saved you one from last night."

"Thank you," Laura said. She dunked the marshmallow up and down, watching it begin to melt. "I've been thinking. I think we'd better change our plans for today."

"You want to head for home this morning?"

"No," Laura said quickly. "Why? Do you think we should?"

"I don't know. I sure don't want to spend another night with an outfit of loony-toonies in the neighborhood."

"I don't either," Laura said. "That's why I figured we'd change plans. The original plan was to leave our gear here today and take a loop to the north. We were supposed to have lunch on the trail and then come back here late in the afternoon."

"And my plan was to sit here all day and wait for you to come back. That's about what I feel like doing."

"But now, with those guys here, I think we can skip that loop and do what I had figured for the third day.

It's about four miles from here to French Lake, but it will take quite a while because it's pretty steep. The trail goes right up that far mountain."

"Sounds like you've got things figured out pretty well. I just got one question: Do you figure that a bunch of squirrels could take their motorcycles to French Lake?"

Laura grinned as she stirred her cocoa. "That's the whole idea. It's a rough trail, rocky and steep. I can't see how they could make it. Besides, I don't think they'd dare. They know it's illegal to have motorcycles in here, and I don't think they'll hang around and wait for a ranger."

"I'll tell you. When it comes to what clowns like those would dare to do, I don't take any bets at all."

"Do you think we ought to head out this morning?" Laura asked sharply. She tried to imagine herself showing up at the Y that afternoon and explaining to her boss why she was back home. She could just picture the I-told-you-so look on his face when she told him that three boys had chased them out.

"I don't know," Irene said. "I'm probably looking for a reason to quit. I'm not much of a camper to start with, I guess. If you figure that trail is too rough for a motorcycle, then we might as well go ahead. I just hope it's not too rough for an old lady that didn't get much sleep last night."

"We'll take it easy," Laura said, relieved that Irene did not insist upon going back.

Irene began to dig through her knapsack. "I better get breakfast going. I can see a couple of tents wiggling. You just figure out what's best, honey. I'll tag along."

Louie Shaw emerged from his tent. "What number do I dial for room service?" he yelled.

By the time the breakfast dishes were washed and all of the gear was packed, it was after nine o'clock. There had been a few grumbles when Laura announced the change of plans, but only Beverly seemed really unhappy. "It's not fair," she kept saying to anybody who would listen. "The only reason we're not going to stay here another night is that Laura doesn't like those guys. And they didn't do a thing wrong. They were as nice as they could be last night. It's just not fair."

While the rest were putting on their packs and adjusting straps, Laura walked quickly to the top of the rise. The trail to French Lake went near the other camp, and she wanted to know whether or not Brian and his crew were awake.

"Are you spying on them?" Beverly said at her shoulder.

Laura turned and faced her. Somehow Beverly had managed to put on her customary mascara and green eye shadow. Laura held back the comments she wanted to make and forced herself to smile. "Mostly I was checking to be sure we hadn't left anything. I also took a look over there, though."

"I don't see why you hate them," Beverly said. Tears began to form in her eyes. "They were real nice last night. They were singing and everything."

"Come on, Bev. Your memory's better than that. You tried to sneak out of your tent to meet Brian last night, and he was there waiting for you. I know you're not happy, but let's keep the facts straight."

Beverly looked at her for a minute, seemed about to speak, then turned and walked back to the others. Laura took one more glance at the far campsite and saw no movement at all.

"Hey, Laura," Louie called, "somebody slipped a load of bricks into my pack."

"Let's move out," Laura said. "It's going to be slow going today. The trail's a little rough. Just take it slow and easy, and you'll do fine."

"Right," Louie yelled. "Go slow and enjoy the pain."

"Chris," Laura said as the others came toward her, "would you lead us for a while?"

Chris grinned. "Sure thing." He stepped ahead, and the others fell into line behind him. He was the ideal pacesetter, steady and deliberate. The most athletic of the group, he could go slowly without being accused of being soft.

As they moved along the trail toward the lakeshore, Laura could see movement in the other camp. Brian crawled out of a sleeping bag, stood up, and stretched. He wore only a pair of jeans. He stretched a second time, but this time, Laura suspected, was for dramatic effect. He had the shoulders and arms of a weight lifter, and he was obviously aware of them.

"Hey," he called, "you guys musta been up early."

"Right," Chris said. He kept on moving.

"Where you going?" Brian asked, walking toward them. Being barefoot, he limped awkwardly over the rocks.

"On up the trail," Chris said.

Beverly stepped off the trail and ran toward Brian, her pack bouncing up and down with each step. "Brian," she called. "Brian, I'm so glad you're awake. I was afraid I wouldn't see you." She ran with her arms stretched out in front of her. Brian stood and watched her come, making no movement toward her. He put a hand on each hip and waited. Beverly slowed her pace, seemed about to stop, and finally reached toward him and gave him a quick hug. He continued to stand with his hands on his hips and said something that Laura couldn't hear.

"I tried, Brian," Beverly said. "I really tried." He shrugged and looked away from her. "I mean it, Brian. I wanted to, but she caught me. She wouldn't let me come." She glared over her shoulder at Laura. "And now we're getting out of here because she doesn't want me around you."

The rest of the hikers had passed. Laura and Irene stood on the trail and waited for Beverly.

"Hi, Laura," Brian said. "How are you this morning?"

"I'm fine."

"Hey, Laura," he said, taking a step in her direction, "tell me something. You're not leaving here because of us, are you?" He rubbed his hands over his bare chest.

"We're going on up the trail," Laura said.

"Yes, she *is*," Beverly said. "We were going to make a day trip with no packs and come back here tonight, but now we're not going to do that."

"Aw, Laura," Brian said, "we didn't mean to scare your little kiddies."

"Come on, Bev," Laura said. "The rest of the bunch is getting ahead of us."

"I don't care," Beverly said.

Laura could sense Irene's growing anger, and she wanted to end the scene before Irene said anything. "Have a good trip, Brian. We have to get moving. We have a long day ahead of us."

"Hey, really, Laura, did we chase you guys off? Are you leaving just to get away from us?"

"Not really," Laura said. "Let's go, Bev."

Beverly put both her hands on Brian's arm. "Yes, really," she said.

"I've had enough of this," Irene shouted. "You featherbrain, you get up on this trail right now and get moving before I give you the spanking that a four-year-old act like this deserves. You get moving right now."

Beverly took a step forward, but Brian reached out and caught her hand. "What's the rush?"

"I've had enough of you too, Tarzan," Irene shouted. "You take your muscles and your motorcycle, and you go bother somebody else for a while. You don't impress me a bit."

"Hey, old lady," Brian yelled, "don't come down on me. I ain't done a thing to you. You just lay off me if you know what's good for you."

"Come on, Bev," Laura said quietly. "The others are a long way ahead by now."

"What's with you people?" Brian asked. "You want to go, go ahead. She'll be along in a minute."

"She's coming right now," Irene said. "You let go of her, or you're gonna have an old lady to deal with."

Brian laughed. "Don't start on me, Grandma. I don't take that stuff. You lay one finger on me, I'll knock you silly. And don't you ever think I won't."

"Oh, I believe you," Irene said. "I know your kind."

"You better believe it. I'm just holding back right now. I already took more off you than I should. One more word out of you, and I'll come right over there and mash your nose. And don't think I won't." His face grew redder as he spoke. "Hey, Laura, I mean it. You get that old bag out of here, or I'll knock her silly. I don't care how old she is."

"Real tough guy," Irene said.

"Irene, please," Laura said quickly. "Will you let me take care of this?"

"You're the boss," Irene said. She glared at all three of them as she marched past.

"Hey, old lady," Brian said more quietly, "it's okay. Don't get so uptight."

Irene turned back to face him. "Go crawl back under your rock. You're nothing but trash. You and your motorcycle and your muscles—you got trash written all over you." She gave her pack a yank and started away.

"You ugly, slimy old bag," Brian yelled. "Just get out of my sight."

"Bev?" Laura asked softly.

"Hey, babe," Brian said to Beverly, "what is this anyway? What's a chick like you doing with a crowd like that? How come you want to go off with that old bag? Or with uptight Laura here?"

"I have to," Beverly said. Laura, relieved, turned away and looked toward the mountain ahead of her.

"No, babe. You don't have to. You got your stuff. You can just stay here with us. We'll take you back home."

Beverly reached out and squeezed his arm. "I can't, Brian."

"Who says? Who says you can't? Some old garbage grandma? Some uptight chick like Laura? They can't make you do what you don't want to do. You just stay here with old Brian. I'll treat you right. It'll be a trip you'll never forget."

"I can't."

"Sure you can, foxy. Nobody can stop you."

"I have to go," Beverly said. She gave Brian's shoulder a pat and turned toward the trail.

"Come kiss me good-bye," he said. "Laura, you gonna watch? You gonna stand there and watch me kiss her good-bye?"

"Not if you hurry," Laura said. She started up the trail, taking slow, measured steps. After fifty steps she stopped and waited. Off to her left she could see Myron sitting by the fire pit. He gave her a quick wave and looked away. A few feet beyond Myron, Wally lay in his sleeping bag, apparently oblivious to all of the noise.

When Laura heard Beverly behind her, she stepped to the side of the trail. "You go ahead."

"All right," Beverly said. "You're the boss." Laura fought off the impulse to respond.

Irene was waiting for them around the first bend in the trail. She let Beverly go past without a word and then stepped in front of Laura. "Sometimes I surprise myself," she said.

"Well, it's over," Laura said.

"I hope so. About the time I start getting into a fight with a musclebound moron, somebody better sign me up for the funny farm."

"It's over," Laura said again.

They had gone only a short distance when Chris, John, and Louie appeared on the trail in front of them. The boys were not wearing their packs. "Everything all right?" Chris called.

"Just fine," Laura answered. "Where are the others?"

"On up the trail. We thought maybe you were having trouble." Chris seemed a little embarrassed.

Laura trotted past Beverly and Irene. "Everything's squared away, boys. But thanks anyway. I appreciate it."

All three of the boys grinned. "I wasn't in the mood for a fight anyway," Louie said. "It's too early in the morning to get my adrenaline pumping."

The trail was steep and rugged and painfully slow. For more than an hour the group climbed steadily upward, stopping to rest every few minutes. Although her legs ached and her throat burned, Laura was happy. She took an almost perverse delight in the tumbled trees and washed-out areas. The trail was rougher than she remembered, and she enjoyed every obstacle on it. It was definitely no trail for a motorcycle.

Even so, when they finally stood at the top of the ridge and looked at the lake far below them, she ignored the panoramic view and tried to reassure herself that Brian and his crew had not moved.

After a long lunch break beside one of the few streams in the area, the group returned to the trail in better spirits. John Gray was in the lead, and he was trying to get the rest of them to sing.

"Forget it, klutzo," his sister said. "Nobody wants to hear you sing."

"Yes, they do," John said. "They're just afraid that you're going to join in. Let's do our theme song." He waved his arm and sang loudly, "You got to walk right up this mountain. You got to walk all by yourself. Nobody else can walk it for you. You got to walk it by yourself."

"Ain't it the truth?" Louie yelled.

"All right," John shouted, "second verse. Louie's got to walk right up this mountain. He's got to walk . . ."

And so it went until everybody's name had been used.

"Enough of this," Irene said. "You'll wear yourselves out."

"Come on," John said. "Let's do 'Sound Off.' "

"Let's not," somebody shouted.

John began to chant. The responses were a little weak, but Laura admired the spirit of anyone who could sing and shout while carrying a full pack.

"On the trail to Fre-ench Lake," John called.

"Sound off," they answered.

"Wondering which trail to— Look out! Look out!"

John crashed into the people behind him, creating a chain reaction which threatened to topple the whole party. Donna began to scream.

Laura dashed forward, unbuckling her pack and letting it slip from her shoulders. She stepped around Chris and Stephanie, shouting, "Move back!" John was looking up the trail, his face greenish white. Laura took his arm and pulled him back against a rock. As she removed his pack, she kept looking for an injury. "Lean back against the rock," she told him, "and then bend over and put your head between your knees."

Irene, suddenly beside Laura, said, "I thought I was

the only nurse in this outfit." She helped steady John as he bent over. "Are you hurt, son?"

"Rattlesnake," John whispered.

Irene was immediately on her knees, lifting his pants legs. "Did it bite you?"

"Nuh-nuh-nuh." John gave up and shook his head as he pushed Irene's hands away.

"That's good," Irene said, letting go of a long breath. "Just lean back and keep your head down. You'll feel better in a minute or two."

Laura looked at the trail in front of them but could see nothing. Donna moved up beside Irene and stood looking at her brother. "You'll do anything for attention, won't you?" she asked softly.

"I'm all right," John said. "I'm all right now."

"Just keep your head down," Irene said. "Don't rush it."

Laura squatted beside him. "John, where was it?"

"By the trail," John said. "Right there in the shade. My foot was right next to it before . . ." His chin began to quiver.

"Thanks, John," Laura said, patting him on the shoulder. As she stood up, she realized that the whole party was crowding in. "Give him a little air, will you? Would you please move back? There's a rattlesnake just ahead, and I'd like to have you put a little space between it and you."

Suddenly everyone was talking, and Laura could

sense the fear in the air. "I'll get him," Chris said, sliding out of his pack.

"Chris, no," Stephanie said, grabbing his arm.

"Just a minute," Laura said loudly. "There's no need to panic. There's a rattlesnake up there—not a bear or a lion. We need a long stick. Louie, will you please go back down the trail and find us a stick?"

"Don't go 'way," Louie said. "I'll be right back." He turned and trotted down the trail.

"Now," Laura said, "if you'll all stay here, I want to go up and see if I can spot it."

"I'll do it," Chris said.

"Let me," Amy said. "Snakes don't bother me."

"I'll do it," Laura said. She started slowly forward. Suddenly every rock and every leaf seemed to look like a snake, and she could feel her whole body growing tense.

John had said that the snake was in the shade, but that was before all of the commotion. As she moved forward, Laura wondered what she would do if they couldn't locate the snake. "It's up there beside that gray boulder," John called out. Laura jumped at the sound of his voice.

The trail at that point was three feet of reasonably flat ground between the rocky face of the hillside and a steep dropoff. As Laura moved forward, she could see the boulder and the small patch of shade it created, but she could see nothing inside that patch. She took another step and another, trying to peer into the darkened area. It wasn't surprising that John had almost stepped on the snake before he realized it was there. That shady spot was a little pocket of darkness in the midst of glaring sunlight.

Then she saw it. Curled into a coil, the snake seemed to be asleep. *Do snakes sleep?* Laura wondered. It was one of those questions that you never think about.

The snake seemed huge. But any coiled snake lying in your path is bound to seem huge. Laura squatted down and peered into the shade. She couldn't distinguish a head. Or a tail, for that matter. At that distance she wasn't positive that it was a rattler and not a gopher snake. The markings of the two were reasonably similar, and she didn't feel like moving in for a closer inspection.

She turned and came back to the group. As she did, she saw Louie coming from the other direction, carrying two long branches—old pine limbs, weathered white. "How are you doing, John?" she asked.

John smiled and shook his head. "I'm all right now. It just scared me. I thought I was going to have a heart attack."

Louie moved past the others and handed Laura one of the two branches. Laura looked at the branch, nearly as tall as she was, and found it uncomfortably short. Would she dare get that close to the snake?

Chris gave Stephanie's shoulder a squeeze and took

the other branch from Louie's hand. "I can go up there and just hold it down with this stick. Then you can use the other stick and some rocks to kill it."

"Oh, no, you don't," Amy said. "That's dumb. There's no reason to kill that snake. All we have to do is move it down the hill and out of our way."

"Oh, sure," Chris said. "And who's going to be the one to move it down the hill? You?"

"Sure," Amy said. "Why not? Give me that stick."

"Amy," Laura said, "do you know what you're doing?"

"Yes. I'm keeping these guys from killing a poor snake. Come on, Chris. Give me the stick."

"I don't care," Chris said as he handed her the branch. "I can do it if you want."

"Never mind," Amy said. "It's not that big a deal." She turned to Laura. "Will you show me where it is, Laura?"

Laura nodded and walked up the trail with her. Once Amy had spotted the snake, she stopped and studied it. "Is anything wrong?" Laura finally asked her.

"No, nothing's wrong. I just don't want to make a mistake. I'm just trying to figure which way to move it. Are you scared, or can you help me?"

"I'm scared," Laura said, "but I can probably help you."

"I'd rather you did it. If Chris does it, I'm afraid he'll panic and hurt the snake."

"I'll try not to panic."

"I guess you think this is dumb, don't you? Trying to protect the snake?"

"No," Laura said, "I don't really think it's dumb. Just be careful. I'd rather not kill the snake, I guess, but I'm a whole lot more concerned about you."

Amy grinned. "Believe it or not, I feel the same way. Now, look, I want to scoot it over on the far side of that boulder and then down the bank. The main thing I want to do is to keep it from crawling into a hole or under something before we get it far enough away. I think the best thing to do is to use this thing like a hockey stick and push the snake along. If it goes in the wrong direction or if I mess up, you can give it a shove. Ready?"

"Just a second," Laura said. "I want to breathe a couple of times first." She closed her eyes and took a long breath. "All right."

"You stay half a step behind me. Don't use your stick unless you have to."

"Don't worry. I'll be perfectly happy to leave it to you."

Amy crept forward toward the shaded spot, her stick held out in front of her. "Get ready now," she whispered.

Suddenly the air was full of a buzzing sound. Laura held tightly to her stick, praying that she would not faint. It seemed incredible that a snake could make that much noise with its tail. As Amy moved her stick into position, the snake suddenly struck at it, extending itself out beyond the shade. Both Amy and Laura instinctively leaped backward.

"Wow," Amy said. "Let's go." She used her stick to rake the snake forward. She kept raking in short, choppy motions, preventing the snake from coiling. Laura moved forward, unable to do anything but watch.

The snake had quit trying to coil. It was moving away from them, sometimes being raked, sometimes wriggling on its own. Amy's stick kept moving, always pushing forward, heading the snake closer and closer to the edge of the embankment.

"Ready now," Amy said. She brought the stick back quickly and moved it forward, intending to send the snake off the path and down the hill. Instead, the stick struck just behind the snake and snapped in two. "Hit it, Laura," Amy shouted as she jumped back.

Laura took one step forward and swung the branch like a golf club. In the middle of her swing, she thought of her follow-through and had a sudden picture of the branch curling around her shoulder. Without realizing what she was doing, she let go of the branch entirely and then stood and watched both branch and snake go sailing over the side.

Amy stood next to the embankment and looked over. "I hope you didn't hurt it," she said.

"Just be glad I don't still have a stick in my hand," Laura said, "or I'd use it on you."

"Oh, Laura," Amy said, "look. It's going off. See. It's

moving just fine. It went down between those two reddish rocks."

"Great," Laura said without looking down.

Together they walked back to where the others were standing. "Let's give a cheer for the snake charmers," Louie yelled.

"I'd rather have a drink of water," Laura said.

"I'd like both," Amy said.

And they gave her both.

IV

"Tell me, kiddo," Irene said. "What do you have planned for tomorrow—Mount Everest?" They were sitting in their damp bathing suits, leaning back against a fallen log.

"Tomorrow we take it easy," Laura said. "We'll pan for gold, and we'll wander over to the other side of the lake. They all want to see the cave over there on the far side of the slide."

"You and the kids go anywhere you want. Me, I think I'll sleep all day. I don't know when I've ever been this beat out."

"I know," Laura said. "I've made that hike before, but I'll swear that it was two miles longer today."

"It's pretty around here, but it's no place for an old lady. I don't know how you ever talked me into this trip in the first place."

Laura looked down at the shoreline, where the others were stretched out on the sand or lying in the shallows. They were an exhausted group, even after a rest and a swim.

The steep trail, together with the heat and the elevation, had worn them down, but the rattlesnake had been the final blow. After seeing that snake, they all had been tense, no matter how they joked. Every crack in the rocks, every shady spot made them uneasy; every movement in the brush was a cause for alarm. The tension and fear had drained the last reserves of energy that any of them might have had.

When they finally crossed the last ridge and looked down on French Lake, their problems had seemed to be over. "Now I know what heaven looks like," Louie had shouted. But the descent had nearly destroyed them—a long mile of switchbacks, often too steep for ordinary walking. It had been torture to have the blue-green water of the lake visible and then to have to pick their way, one slow step at a time, down the steep trail.

Laura had intended to camp on the far side of the lake, but she had abandoned that plan in the middle of the descent. The group had taken the first path off the main trail and stopped at the first place to camp. Fortunately it was a good campsite, but they would have stayed there anyway.

Although she was as tired as the rest, Laura was content. Under her leadership the Y group had succeeded. They had made it to French Lake, the destination they had selected at the planning session two weeks before. Besides, there was a yellow tent set up in the area where she had originally intended to camp, and there was a fisherman by the rockslide. And camp was set up. She had insisted, after an hour of swimming, that the tents be put up and wood gathered. Now they could relax in peace. Their mission was accomplished, their chores were finished, the lake was beautiful, and there was company. It was no wonder that she felt a sense of satisfaction that helped soothe her aching muscles.

"Laura! Laura!" It took Laura a minute to realize where she was. She opened her eyes far enough to see Amy standing over her. "They're coming! Those hoods are coming. I can hear the engines."

Laura stood up slowly, stretching out her sore arms. She felt like Rip Van Winkle waking up from his twenty-year sleep. "How long have I been asleep?"

Amy looked at her disapprovingly. "I don't know. Not very long. Can't you hear them?" Laura merely nodded. "They're going to be here in just a few minutes. What are you going to do?"

"I'm going to go down to the lake and wash my face and try to wake up." Amy stood and stared. "If you'd gather everybody together, I'd appreciate it."

Amy's face softened. "Sure."

Laura pulled on her sandals and walked to the edge of the lake. On a sudden impulse she kicked off her shoes and took two steps into the icy water before holding her breath and plunging in. She swam a few strokes as her whole body rebelled against the shock.

Then she turned and waded back to her shoes. She had no easy answers, but at least she was awake now.

By the time she reached the campsite, the others were gathered around the fire pit. The noise of the motors was louder, and she kept watching the main trail where it circled the lake, expecting to see the cycles come into view. "They're here," she said, keeping her voice quiet and calm. As if to confirm the point, one of the cycles appeared on the trail they had been watching. "I didn't think they could make it here, but obviously I was wrong. I think the best way to handle things is for us not to have anything to do with them. I think you can see that we have a tricky situation here."

"Oh, come on," Beverly said. "Why don't you just say it?"

"You'd better be listening," Irene told her.

Laura shook her head at Irene. "I *have* said it. We aren't going to have anything to do with them."

"They haven't done anything," Beverly said, her mouth forming a pout.

"You know better than that."

"Not one thing," Beverly insisted.

"Threatening to beat up Irene doesn't count?" Laura asked quickly.

"But that was after she started calling Brian names. What do you expect after she acts like that?" Irene stared up at the sky.

"Let's cool it, Bev," Chris said quietly.

Beverly turned toward him and began to cry. "That's easy for you to say. There you are, you and Steff, what do you care? It's just not fair."

"Come on, Bev," Stephanie said. She put a hand on Beverly's shoulder.

"I don't care," Beverly said. "It's just not fair, and you all know it." She shook off Stephanie's hand and walked away from the circle.

"Fair or not," Laura said, "that's the way it's going to be. I'm sorry if it makes some of you unhappy."

"Poor Donna," John said. "She thought the big dude with the beard was cute."

"Why don't you go step on a snake?" Donna said.

"All right," Laura said, "let's get some kindling and start a fire."

"I still don't think it's fair," Beverly called back. "You never did like me, and now you're just getting back at me." She turned away and marched down to the lake.

While kindling was being stacked and the fire started, Laura wandered down by the water's edge, keeping her eye on the far shore. Beverly made a point of walking away when Laura came near.

Laura wished that she had brought a pair of binoculars. It was probably no more than a quarter mile across the lake, but that was too far for her to see much. Two figures appeared along the shore, moving beside the yellow tent. A minute or two later both the figures and the tent were gone. Laura continued to watch, but there was nothing more to see.

Finally, tired of watching a blank shoreline, she wandered back to where Irene was starting supper. "I don't know about you," Irene said, "but I could have done without company."

"I'm so sorry we didn't go back to our cars today," Laura said.

"That's history, honey. If I want history, I read a book. We just won't have anything to do with them."

"I hope it works that way."

"I'm about ready to put a leash on that Beverly and keep hold of it all night."

"At least we have some other people around," Laura said. "I hated it last night when there was nobody else around at all." She kept watching the far shore, hoping to see the yellow tent appear once more.

A few minutes later, while she was again scanning the far shore, Laura spotted a pair of hikers coming along the main trail beside the lake. It was silly, of course, but as Laura saw the hikers headed in her direction, she thought of those old movies where the cavalry appears just in time to save the wagon train. She stopped by the campsite long enough to tell Irene where she was going, then hurried toward the trail junction to wait for them. No matter who they were, she would be happy to have them close by.

As the pair approached her, Laura called out a

cheery hello. The hiker closest to her, a man in his forties, smiled. The other hiker, probably his wife, said, "Good afternoon."

"There's a nice campsite just down this way," Laura said.

"We're going on to Jack Pine Lake," the man said, not even slowing down as he walked past her.

"That's quite a hike for this time of day," Laura said.

"We'll make it."

Laura watched them go by, then shouted, "Could you wait just a minute? I'm sorry. I don't know what to do. There are some boys on motorcycles here, and we're a little frightened."

The man stopped and looked back at her. "I know. They came in next to us and started making noise and swearing. When I spoke to them, they got really nasty. I don't need that."

"You were the ones with the yellow tent?" Laura asked weakly.

"That's right. We were here for three days—very peaceful. And then these troublemakers show up."

"We're a little frightened," Laura said.

"You'd better get out, too," the man told her. "Just leave troublemakers like that alone. There's nothing else to do." He shifted his pack and started walking.

"Look," Laura said, "I have a Y group here. Couldn't you stay with us tonight? Then we could all go out in the morning."

"If you know what's best, you'll take them out of here tonight. I'm sorry. I don't come up here for things like this. You take my advice. You just leave trouble-makers like that alone. It's the only thing to do."

Laura stood helplessly as the two hurried off. The woman looked back over her shoulder once and seemed about to speak but then turned away.

"Irene," Laura said as soon as she returned to camp, "those were the people camped across the lake. They were leaving to get away from Brian and his pals. That means there's nobody else up here—just us and them. I think we'd better gather our gear and head out."

"It's already close to six o'clock. Do you figure we can get packed up and make it back to Jack Pine by dark?"

"I think we'd better give it a try."

"This crowd is plenty spooked about snakes right now. They're gonna be real skittery when it starts getting dark."

"I know," Laura said, "but I hate to think of having Brian and his crew around for another night."

Irene looked at her and shook her head. "Me, too. But if those jokers followed us all the way in here, don't you think they'd follow us back out again? Especially if they figured out we were running from 'em."

"Maybe," Laura said quickly, "but we can't just sit here."

"I know how you feel, but there's just one thing I better tell you—I don't think I can make it back out of here today. I'm just about out of gas. I'm not used to this kind of stuff, and I don't have much hiking left in me right now."

"All right," Laura said. "We'll stay here then. We'll manage."

"Sure we will, honey. All we have to do is tie Beverly to a tree."

After the dinner dishes were cleaned and more wood had been gathered, the group stood around the campfire. The camp was in shadows, although the tops of the mountains across the lake were still lighted by the sun. Irene was handing out cups of lemonade. "This stuff wouldn't be too awful," she said, "if you'd never had real lemonade. But it's something to drink, I guess. Me, I think I'll stick to coffee."

"Ah," Louie said, "my favorite flavor—preservatives."

"Listen," Amy said. "Do you hear something?"

Once everyone was quiet, the sounds of the motorcycle engines came bouncing across the lake. "Just those little boys playing with their toys," Irene said.

"Let's go ahead and sing," Laura said. "Why don't we start with 'Midnight Special'?"

"Look," Amy said, "they're coming. If you look over where the trail comes out by those willows, you can see them."

"That's all right," Laura said as calmly as she could. "Let's go ahead and sing."

The verses of "Midnight Special" became increasingly weak as the motorcycles circled the lake. Laura stopped in mid-verse when she realized that only she and Irene were still singing. "All right," she said. "They'll be here in a minute. I'm going to tell them that we'd like to be left alone, and that'll be it. It would be easier for me if the rest of you would go on singing."

"Let me go with you, Laura," Chris said.

"No. I think it's better if I go by myself."

"I still don't think . . ." Beverly began.

"Oh, shut up," Amy said.

"Let's try our theme song," Irene shouted. "I want to do it standing still for a change." She began to sing, and some of the others joined in halfheartedly. Laura turned away from the fire and walked down the path, past the boys' tents, toward the oncoming cycles.

Brian came toward her slowly, weaving along the narrow path. He stopped directly in front of her and turned off his motor. The other two stopped behind him. Only Myron was wearing his crash helmet.

"Hi, Laura," Brian said with an easy smile. "What's happening?"

"Hello, Brian." She forced herself to smile.

"Sounds like your singing needs some help. It's a little weak right now."

"We're doing all right," Laura said.

"Well, we're just what the doctor ordered. We'll put a little life into things." He swung his leg over the bike and pushed it back onto its kickstand.

"Brian, I'd rather you didn't join us tonight."

"Come on, Laura. What's the trouble? You mad about this morning? If I did something wrong, I'm sorry. Know what I mean? I'm sorry. I'll even tell that old lady I'm sorry if you want, even if she *was* the one that started it."

"I just think it would be better if you didn't join us," Laura said.

He looked at her, no longer smiling. "Look, Laura, we had a rough time getting here. Maybe you didn't notice, but that wasn't exactly a freeway coming into here. You think we're gonna come all this way, hauling our bikes over the rough spots and everything, and then not even come to visit? Come on, Laura. We've had a rough day. Let's be friendly and easy. It's the best way. You know what I mean? There's other ways, Laura, and you better believe it. But friendly and easy is the best way."

Behind her, Laura could hear "On Top of Old Smokey," with Irene's voice much stronger than any other. "You're right, Brian," she said. "Let's keep it friendly and easy. You take that side of the lake, and we'll take this side. I think things will work out better that way."

"Well, see, Laura, I don't. So there we are. You figure I oughta go back and sit around my campfire, and I figure I oughta come over here and sit by yours. So now what? Where do we go from here, Laura?"

"There's no use continuing this."

"I'll tell you what, Laura. I don't care all that much for singing. I mean, it's all right. It's kind of fun once in a while. But I can live without it. But, see, that little Beverly's different. I came to see her, came all the way up that dumb cow path—hauling my bike up and down those hills, pushing almost as much as riding. And now I want to see her. So, if you don't want us at your campfire, that's all right. Then Beverly can come and visit ours."

"You know I can't let her go," Laura said.

"Well, then, I guess we come to your fire." He looked back over his shoulder. "Wally, you ready to sing?"

"Sure," Wally said.

"Let's go then."

Laura backed up to keep between them and the fire. "You aren't welcome here." She knew how silly that sounded.

Brian laughed loudly. "Now, Laura, you're gonna hurt my feelings talking that way." He looked over his shoulder. "Come on, Wally. Let's go sing." Wally leaned his bike against a tree and came toward them. Myron removed his helmet but continued to straddle his machine.

The singing at the campfire had died out along with the engines, and Laura could sense all of them watching her. "Please, Brian," she said softly. "Please leave us alone."

"We're not gonna hurt anything," Brian said. He

moved around her and marched toward the campfire. "Hey, everybody, let's do some more singing." He strode into the middle of the group. "Hi, Bev, you little fox." He grabbed her shoulder, pulled her toward him, and kissed her squarely on the mouth. "Hey, now that's what I came for."

Beverly smiled weakly but made no move either toward him or away from him. The others stood around the fire, uneasy, like people who have stopped at an automobile accident. Wally came up to the fire and began to rub his hands together. Myron remained with his motorcycle.

"Come on, Laura," Brian said, his arm around Beverly. "Let's have a song."

"The singing is over for tonight," Laura said evenly.

"Well, then, we better have a second session. You guys are ready to sing some more, aren't you?" Nobody answered him. "How about you, foxy? You want to sing, don't you?"

Beverly smiled and looked down at the fire. "I don't know," she said, breaking into a giggle. "I guess so."

"Okay, then we're gonna have some more singing. What this little fox wants, she gets. So we're gonna sing."

Laura stood and watched, unable to decide what to do. Irene, she noticed, had disappeared from the circle. Myron had left his bike but still stood back in the shadows.

"The singing is over for tonight," Laura said again.

"No, it isn't," Brian said. "We decided to sing some more. If you don't want to join us, you can go somewhere else. The rest of us, we're getting ready to sing. Come on, Myron. Get in here and give us a hand."

"I'm okay," Myron said.

"What you need," Brian said, "is to get your arm around one of these little foxes. It makes you feel like singing."

Laura could sense all three of the girls drawing away. Chris had moved in front of Stephanie, and Laura spoke quickly, hoping to head him off. "Brian," she said, trying to keep her voice friendly, "you've had your joke. Now we're going to have prayers, and we'd like to have quiet."

"It's not time for beddie-bye," Brian shouted. "It's not even dark. You wanta go say prayers, that's cool. Go somewhere else and pray all you want to. We're busy here."

"Why don't you clear out of here?" Chris said. He was standing about three feet from Brian, with his fists doubled.

Brian smiled and shook his head. "I don't know about you guys. You're not a real friendly bunch." He took his arm off Beverly's shoulder. "What do you say, Wally? I get the idea that some of these people don't like us. You think we oughta go?" He took a step toward the campfire, not looking in Chris's direction. "I guess the kid here has a point. You know what I mean?" He suddenly turned and buried his fist into Chris's solar plexus. The punch was finished before any of them suspected it was coming.

Chris tumbled to the ground and began making gasping noises. "Chris!" Stephanie screamed and dropped to her knees beside him.

"What are you doing?" Laura shouted, moving between Brian and Chris.

Louie and John moved toward Brian, but Wally stepped in their way, his head lowered. "You stay out of it," Wally growled. Louie and John looked at each other but stayed where they were. Myron moved a few steps closer to the fire.

"He's all right," Brian said, turning toward the fire. "He just has the wind knocked out of him. It doesn't matter. He wasn't much of a singer anyway."

"Brian!" Beverly said, moving away from him. "You didn't have to . . ."

Brian reached for her and pulled her roughly toward him. "Hey, foxy, don't talk. Girls like you are made for looking at—not for talking. You just remember that, and we'll get along fine." He gave her shoulders a squeeze. "Now we're gonna have a song."

"But, Brian . . ." Beverly began.

"I told you to shut up, foxy. Nobody wants to hear you talk. Now let's all sing."

"Brian," Laura said as she bent over Chris, "won't you please leave?"

"You got a hearing problem, Laura. We're gonna sing. You people haven't been very friendly, and you'd better start changing your ways if you know what's good for you. I told you before. The best way is the friendly, easy way. But it's not the only way. So don't start asking for trouble, or you'll be sorry."

Laura knelt down beside Stephanie. Chris was beginning to breathe without gasping, but he continued to lie where he had fallen. Stephanie ran her hands through his hair and sobbed.

"Okay," Brian said, "we're gonna sing that 'Kumbayah' thing we did last night, and we're all gonna sing. Anybody that doesn't sing, they're gonna make me and Wally mad. And that's a bad thing to do. So everybody better gather around and sing nice and loud. You, too, Laura. And that little fox with the tears running down her face."

"Leave us alone," Stephanie shouted. "Just leave us alone."

Brian slipped his arm off Beverly's shoulder and walked slowly toward Stephanie. "Two ways to go, cutie. Either you can sing with us when I ask you to." He moved next to Stephanie, who kept her eyes lowered. "Or else you can make me mad. And if I get mad, somebody's going to get hurt." He drove a foot into Chris's back. "Like that."

"Brian!" Laura shouted. John plunged forward, but Wally shoved him away roughly and held up a warning finger.

"Don't!" Stephanie screamed. "What's the matter with you?"

Brian caught her by the arm and pulled her to her feet. "What's the matter with you, cutie? Why can't you do things the easy way? I tell you to sing—you sing. Or do you want to find out how tough your boyfriend is?" He kicked Chris once again.

"Let's sing," Laura said, standing up and moving into the circle. "Let's all sing."

"See, cutie," Brian said. "That's the easy way. But girls like you don't always learn the easy way." He ran his boot along Chris's spine. Chris continued to lie in the same position. "What do you say? You want to keep going, or you want to start being sensible?"

Stephanie tightened her trembling jaw. "Let's sing," she said. "Please. Can we sing?"

Brian laughed and bowed to the fire. "See? See how easy it is? I keep telling you. It's better to do things the easy way." He walked past Laura and stood beside Beverly once more.

"Brian," Beverly said, "can't you—"

"Shut up, foxy. I get sick of you whining." He put a hand on her shoulder and pulled her toward him. "Now we're gonna do that 'Kumbayah' thing, and we're all gonna sing."

In spite of her fear and anger, Laura could not help noting the irony of singing a hymn in these circumstances. As she joined the others in singing, "Someone needs you, Lord. Kumbayah," she marveled at the appropriateness of the words.

They stood in a circle and sang. John and Louie

stared into the fire, looking at no one. Myron stood a step or two behind them. Chris continued to lie where he had fallen, although Laura noticed that his breathing now seemed normal enough. She hoped that he would stay where he was.

"That was pretty good," Brian said when they finished. "I knew you guys really felt like singing. Now let's do that one you did last night—that hammer song. Get us started, Laura."

Laura began "Take This Hammer," and the others joined in. As they moved into the second verse, Wally moved past John and stood next to Amy. Amy began to edge away from him, leaning toward Donna. Wally looked down at her and grinned. He seemed gigantic standing next to her. Amy kept moving away, but he followed each of her edging steps with one of his.

"Hold it," Brian yelled in the middle of a verse. The song stopped immediately. "Cut it out. You're messing up the circle. You," he said, pointing at Amy, "you stay where you belong. Wally, you put your arm around her just to be sure she does."

"If you say so," Wally said with a grin.

"Don't you touch me," Amy shouted.

"Hey, pint-size," Brian said, "you better think a minute. You better just shut up and think a minute. If I was you, I'd be nice to Wally. He can be a real good friend to you, and you just might need a real good friend. Know what I mean?"

"You don't scare me," Amy shouted. "Guys like you,

you think you're tough, but you don't scare me." She turned to Wally. "You keep your filthy hands off me." Wally looked at her and smiled.

"Brian," Beverly said, "don't make her—"

"I told you to shut up, foxy. Nobody wants to listen to you whine."

"What a neat boyfriend you got," Amy shouted at Beverly. "I just hope you're satisfied."

Just then Irene called from the far side of the tents, "Would you guys like something to eat? I've got some hot cocoa and cookies if you want them."

Brian laughed. "That'd be great," he called. "See? That old lady's wised up. That's the way to do things. Friendly and easy. You treat us nice, and we'll treat you nice." He gave Beverly's shoulder a squeeze. "Relax, foxy. Tonight I'm gonna treat you real nice. You just wait." He looked over at Amy and grinned. "So you're a mean one, huh? You'd better learn your lesson in a hurry, half-pint, or you're gonna be sorry for a long time to come."

Amy glared back at him but said nothing.

Laura began to sing "When the Saints Go Marching In," and the rest joined in. Laura was not certain what Amy would do next, and it seemed better to delay. Brian smiled at her, apparently happy that she was leading songs once more. Wally moved close to Amy, who leaned away from him. "Don't touch me," she said quietly.

He put his arm around her shoulders. "That doesn't

hurt, does it?" The top of her head came to the middle of his chest.

"It makes my stomach hurt," Amy said, but she didn't move. She stood with her shoulders rigid, like a soldier at attention, and tears streamed down her cheeks.

While she sang, Laura kept watching Irene. She knew the old woman well enough not to take the surrender at face value. Something was going to happen. Laura was certain of that. In the meantime, all she could do was keep singing.

Chris was sitting up now, a few feet behind the others. He was still pale, but he seemed to be steadier. At the end of the song Brian turned toward Chris and said, "Hey, come get in the circle."

"Can't," Chris moaned.

"Look, turkey, I told you to come get in the circle. Now you better do it. Otherwise, Wally and I are gonna come over there and help you."

Chris rose to his feet and staggered toward the fire. Laura was certain, watching him, that Chris was not as weak as he was pretending to be.

"You sit down right there," Brian told him. "You and you"—pointing to John and Louie—"move over and sit on each side of him." The two of them came around the circle quickly. "Now we can all sit down." Brian waited until everyone but Myron was seated and then walked around the circle. Myron stepped back and let him pass. "See? This is nice and easy. No problems, no trouble." He moved behind Chris, who turned toward him. "Turn around, turkey. Look at the fire." Chris did not move. "If you don't turn around, you're gonna be sorry. And don't try to stand up, or I'll toss you right into that fire." Chris slowly turned away. "That's better." Brian stepped forward and drove his boot into Chris's back. Chris grunted and sagged forward. "Next time don't make me ask twice." He moved behind Louie. "What about you, tubby? You want some?" He nudged Louie with the toe of his boot.

"No," Louie said, still facing the fire.

"Call me sir," Brian said. "Show a little respect."

"Let's sing," Laura pleaded. "There's no need for this. Let's go ahead and sing."

"All right, Laura," Brian said. "But first he's going to say 'sir,' aren't you, fat boy?" He nudged Louie again.

"Yessir," Louie said.

"What was that?"

"Yes, sir."

"All right, Laura. Now we can sing. And I want everybody to sing nice and loud." He walked back and sat beside Beverly, who shifted away from him. "What's this?" he shouted. "Don't you start in, foxy. You're gonna make me mad, too, and then where'll you be?" He put an arm around her shoulder and yanked her toward him. "Don't you ever move away from me. You hear me? Don't you ever do that again." Beverly looked around at the others, then looked into the fire.

Laura began "Michael, Row the Boat Ashore," and

the rest followed. Irene came to the fire, placed a cup of cocoa and a plate of cookies in front of Wally and Amy, and walked away. Wally immediately reached for a cookie with his free hand. As the verses continued, Irene appeared and reappeared, bending over each of them to place the plates on the ground.

Laura tried not to stare at Irene. Irene had to be planning something, but Laura could not figure what it could be. Meanwhile, all she could do was keep the singing going and wait. When she could think of no more verses to "Michael," she immediately began "Clementine." Wally was busy with his cookies, but the others kept singing.

Irene moved around the circle, setting out plates and cups like a well-trained waitress. Brian sang vigorously, his eyes moving around the circle continuously. The others avoided his glances by staring into the fire. Laura kept her voice steady and waited.

Irene bypassed Laura and Donna and set a plate in front of Beverly. Then, standing directly behind Brian, she handed him a plate and cup. As he took them, Irene moved back a few inches, then grabbed his hair and yanked him backward. The plate and cup clattered to the ground.

"Nobody move," Irene shouted, "or I'll cut his throat." Only then did Laura see the knife that Irene held just below Brian's ear. "All right, buddy. You tell your two pals to hop on their motorcycles and clear out of here. I'm a nurse, and I know right where the artery is."

"Come on," Brian began. His body was bent backward, helplessly off-balance, held upright only by his hair.

"You do what I tell you," Irene said. "And quick."

Wally sat watching, still absently munching on a cookie. Amy pulled away from him, but he seemed not to notice. He continued to stare at Irene, as if waiting for an explanation. Myron was already walking back toward the cycles.

"You guys go ahead and get out of here," Brian said. Wally got up slowly and walked away from the fire. "Go ahead, Wally. I'll see you back at camp."

As soon as the motorcycle engines started, Irene began to shout. "All right, somebody get me some rope, and hurry up about it." She shifted her position slightly and gave Brian's hair a tug. "Just don't start wiggling. I'm an old lady with shaky hands."

"This is crazy," Brian said. "We were just playing around."

"Me, too, pal. But old ladies play rough."

Louie came back with a piece of cord that must have come from a sleeping bag. "Is this all right?"

"It's a start," Irene said. "Get in and tie his hands behind him."

"Come on," Brian said. "You don't have to tie me up."

"Make the knots good and tight," Irene told Louie. "I don't want to have to sit here with my knife all night."

Laura watched the headlights of the motorcycles bounce and weave through the brush. Wally and Myron were heading straight back to the other camp. What they would do then, she could not begin to guess.

"Get his shoelaces and tie his feet together," Irene said. "First do his ankles and then his knees."

"Listen," Brian said, "this is crazy. You don't have to do this."

"Yeah, but it's kind of fun," Irene said.

Louie and John made short work of Brian's ankles and knees, using both his shoelaces and his belt. Only then did Irene get up and put away her knife. "That ought to do you. Now just one more thing: I don't want to have a lot of trouble tonight, so when your pals get over there at the camp and shut off their cycles, you're gonna yell over and tell 'em to stay where they are. You're gonna tell 'em to stay right over there and to be ready to answer if we call. Otherwise, we're gonna make life real unpleasant for you. You got that?"

"Forget it, old lady," Brian said. "There's no way in the world you're gonna make me yell anything. I'm gonna have you arrested for kidnapping." Irene snorted. "They'll be back over here to help me. You wait and see. And you're gonna be sorry you ever started this. You just wait and see."

Laura called Irene and moved away from the fire. "Wow," she said, "you really came through."

"The question is, honey: Did I make things better or worse? I don't know for sure. The way that maniac was carrying on, I figured things couldn't get any worse. Now I'm not so sure. I wonder if we can keep him tied up until we get back to our cars."

"I don't know," Laura said. She looked at her group, huddled around the fire and watching Brian. Then she looked across the lake where the motorcycle headlights were still bouncing.

"I'll tell you one thing," Irene said. "I got a feeling this is going to be a long night."

V

Nobody wanted to go to sleep that night. The thought that Wally might be crawling around somewhere was enough to keep all of them close to the fire. After a long period of quiet, when things were gradually settling down, Brian began to taunt them. "I think he's coming. Listen. You can hear those big old feet clumping through the brush. When Wally's mad, nothing can stop him. And you can bet he's mad right now. He's gonna come in here and start throwing bodies up into the trees. All except you, half-pint. He likes you. When he's all done with the rest, he'll take you back to camp with him."

"Can't we shut him up?" Amy asked.

"That's enough," Irene told him. "You're all through talking. If you want, I can get some tape for your mouth. I got a whole first-aid kit full of it."

"You're the one, old lady," Brian shouted. "You're the one I'm gonna get."

"Don't feel bad, sonny. You're not the first punk that got whipped by an old woman."

Brian began to swear at her, his voice getting louder and louder.

Irene came close enough to him to put her foot on his back. "One more word, and I'll get the tape."

He rolled over enough to look up at her. "What kind of old lady are you anyhow? I'm tied up and can't do a thing, and you keep picking on me."

"I'll be right back," Irene said. She walked to her tent and came back in a minute with a roll of tape.

"All right," Brian said as she approached. "I won't talk anymore. I'll keep quiet. You don't have to use that stuff."

"I'll keep it handy just in case. One smart word out of you, and on it goes."

Laura sat and stared into the darkness. Donna Gray, sitting next to her, was nodding forward, eyes closed. Louie's head was down on his chest. "Hey, gang," Laura said, "as long as you feel like staying around the fire, why don't you go get your sleeping bags and bring them here?" One or two people stood up, but nobody moved away from the fire. "What you ought to do is all go together. Just stop at each tent and get what you need."

The whole group trooped off toward the tents. Irene signaled for Laura to move away from the fire with her. "Well, Laura," she muttered when they were far enough away that Brian couldn't hear, "you got any good ideas?"

"Not really."

"All my good ideas come too late. While we had those bozos here, we should have gotten them all tied up. Or we should have taken away their shoes or something."

"That's not a bad idea," Laura said. "About the shoes, I mean."

"Yeah, but it's history now. I feel like the guy with the lion by the tail. We're all right for the moment, but it's hard to figure out how to let go." She shook her head, and Laura thought she saw a tear begin to form. "I guess I got going too fast, honey. I just didn't know what else to do."

"Look, Irene, at least our kids are okay. And they weren't before. We'll just see what happens at daylight. If we can get a good jump, we can probably beat them back to Jack Pine Lake. All we need to do is mess up the trail in a few spots." She hoped that Irene wouldn't ask why Jack Pine Lake would be any safer than where they were. Laura had no answer for that.

"Oh, Lordy," Irene said, her voice trembling a little.

"Or else there's the rockslide over there. If worse comes to worst, we can go up that slide. They sure can't follow us up there on their bikes."

"Where's this rockslide?"

"Down that way. Didn't you see it when we were swimming today? The whole west side of the lake is boulders."

"I was so tired today I wasn't noticing anything."

"Well, it's there anyway. I've never been up it, but

I know people who have. Cold Springs Lake is on the other side of the ridge from here. It's about eight miles to that lake by the trail, and some people go up and over the rockslide instead."

"I know what I'll do," Irene said. "I'll make that ape carry my pack. That's about the only way I'll make it."

As the group came back carrying sleeping bags, there was no talk at all. Laura watched each of the faces and could find only fear and exhaustion and resignation. As the sleeping bags were spread out, each one was arranged so that it was touching the others. Without any discussion the group had decided to move away from the fire so that they could stay closer together. When the arrangements were complete, the bags were in a small circle, all of the heads inward.

"Looks like a flower," Irene muttered.

"Try to get some sleep," Laura told the others as they climbed into their sleeping bags. "We're going to be leaving here at daylight. Even if you can't sleep, lie in your bag and let your muscles relax. Just try to float free. If you do that, it's almost as good as sleep." Besides, if they did that, they would probably fall asleep immediately.

"You better sleep a little right now yourself," Irene said. "I'm too wired up to sleep right away. I'll wake you up when I start to drift."

Laura brought the two sleeping bags from their tent. She wondered uneasily if she was being watched. After seeing Brian huddled on the ground, she made a second trip to the tent and brought her air mattress. "Come on," she said disgustedly. She helped him roll onto the mattress, then covered him with the blanket from the first-aid kit.

"There's no sense in this," he said. "You just let me go, and I'll go back to my camp, and that'll be the end of it. I don't want anything more to do with you people."

Laura turned away, not bothering to answer. "You just be glad she got you a mattress and blanket," Irene said, pulling her sleeping bag around her. "That's more than I would have done. You brought this on yourself. You remember that tonight."

"I'll remember you, old lady. And you'll wish I hadn't."

"I still have that tape right here."

Laura crawled into her bag and wiggled her toes against the cold. The ground was uneven, and it was hard to find a spot where her bones weren't rubbing against something hard. She began to relax her muscles, determined to get what rest she could. Two minutes later she was sound asleep.

When Irene patted her cheek to wake her, Laura rose up with a start. "It's all right, honey. I just can't keep my eyes open any longer. You better take over."

"What time is it?" Laura asked.

"A little after twelve."

"I've been asleep longer than I thought."

"I wish I could have given you more, but I'm all in."

"Go ahead and go to sleep, Irene. I'll be fine."

Irene unzipped her sleeping bag, pulled it around her, and was silent. Laura sat up and looked around. The night air was cool, and she hated to pull herself all the way out of her bag. She sat and looked across the lake. Except for the reflection of the moon and stars on the lake, she could see nothing.

When she finally pulled herself out of the sleeping bag and slipped on her boots, Laura found herself much more uneasy. There was a security in that bag that went beyond mere warmth. She stood up quickly and moved to the fire, where she pushed together the logs that were left and added another. She held her wrist toward the fire and saw that it was twelve thirty. That meant that it had been almost three hours since Wally and Myron had gone off. How long would they wait at their camp? She listened for several minutes but could hear only the usual night sounds and the sizzling and popping of the fire.

"Hey, Laura." It was only a whisper, but she jumped at the sound. She turned to see Brian looking at her.

"Just go back to sleep," she said, turning away.

"Hey, look, I'm sorry. I mean it. I'm sorry I caused all this trouble."

"Great," Laura said sarcastically. "You're sorry now. So that takes care of it all, huh?"

"What can I say? I already said I'm sorry."

"Well, so am I. So go to sleep."

"Hey, I didn't mean for it to happen the way it did. I was mad when you wouldn't let us sing. We weren't gonna cause any trouble."

"Come on."

"So, all right. Maybe we were. But I was mad, and then things got crazy. Know what I mean? I didn't really mean to hit that kid. It was just a sucker punch, and I did it before I thought. The whole thing was a bad scene, and I wish it hadn't happened."

"So do I."

"It's crazy, you know. I get started into things, and before I know it, it's like somebody else is doing the things. And all I'm doing is hanging on for the ride. You ever felt like that?"

"I don't know."

"Well, it's like it's not really me doing the things. But it *is* me. Aw, forget it. I'm sorry about the whole thing."

"Well, so am I. So go back to sleep."

"Look, it's over. You got me. What else do you want?"

"What I really want is for you to be quiet. I don't have anything to say to you."

"All right," he said slowly. "I won't bother you anymore."

"Good."

"But, look, will you do one thing for me? I'm about to freeze to death. Do you have anything that . . . ?" His voice trailed off. "I know. I got no right to ask."

"No, you don't," Laura said. "I'll put my sleeping bag over you for a while." She brought her bag and laid it carefully over the other blanket. "How's that?"

"Great. Thanks, Laura. I really mean it. I was freezing." He lay quietly for a minute. "Yeah, this is better. I'll be all right now. If I could just . . . I'll be all right."

Laura sat and poked at the fire.

"Look," Brian said, "I hate to keep bothering you, but . . ."

"What now?"

"I'm sorry, Laura, but my left leg's gone to sleep, and I can't seem to move enough to get the blood going to it. You think you could loosen things up a little? I don't mean untie me or anything. Just loosen this one rope a little."

Laura stood up. "And then I suppose you'll want a pillow." She took a step toward him, then stopped abruptly. "I'm lousy with knots. As soon as somebody else wakes up, I'll get them to do it."

"Come on, Laura. I'm hurting. You want me to beg? I will if you want me to. I'll beg you."

"Can you wait a while? I hate to wake anybody."

"All I need is for you to loosen this one knot. It's no big deal. Come on. Help me out. My leg's really getting bad."

"I'll wake somebody up," she said finally.

"Don't do that. It's not worth it. I just need one little rope loosened. Is that too much to ask?"

Laura walked over to where he lay. She pulled back

the sleeping bag and the blankets. Brian lay on his side, looking up at her. She looked down at the laces wrapped around Brian's knee, trying to make out the knots. "I think I'll wake somebody up," she said, dropping the bag over Brian again.

Brian began to laugh. "You're too much, Laura. You're so sneaky I don't even have a chance. I think I've got you going, giving you all this 'I'm sorry' crud, and you're just waiting for me. Why didn't you tell me to save my breath?"

"I did. Besides, I thought maybe you really were sorry. You have plenty of reason to be."

"Come on. I was just trying to con you, and you knew it from the start. Now leave me alone and let me sleep."

Laura sat by the fire and stared into the darkness, grateful for the silence. Brian was wrong. She hadn't been sure he was trying to con her. After all, she had given him her sleeping bag, and she had come very close to helping him with the ropes. *I'm a born sucker*, she thought.

She looked over at the circle of sleeping bags, the heads resting only inches from each other. Those people were depending on her, and she had almost made a foolish mistake, one that could have endangered all of them. Reaching into her pocket, she wrapped her hand around the cold metal of her knife.

Laura jerked her head up and looked around. Her

neck was sore, and she was cold. Once she was sure that nobody was coming, she looked at her watch. It was almost two o'clock. She had slept for over half an hour. She stood up quickly and put a stick on the fire, thankful that her negligence hadn't cost them anything. She didn't dare sit again. She had been lucky twice already, and she wasn't going to take any more chances.

Then she heard it, a crashing and tumbling sound behind her. A rock maybe. It was hard to tell. But it was noise, unnatural noise. "Irene," she called. "Irene." She stood by the fire, peering out toward the noise. Someone was moving out there, no longer trying to be silent.

Irene was immediately out of her sleeping bag and beside Laura. "What is it, Laura?"

"Somebody's out there."

Irene pulled the sleeping bag off Brian and shook his shoulder. "Wake up, Sleeping Beauty."

"Go 'way," Brian groaned.

The crashing in the brush grew louder, and Laura could hear the individual steps. "Do you hear that?"

"I hear it," Irene said. "Hey," she yelled, slapping Brian lightly, "you tell those pals of yours to get out of here, or I'll make you a foot shorter."

Brian came up off the ground. "I didn't do anything," he shouted.

Irene grabbed him. "Call off your friends. Right now."

Laura could see the faint outline of someone moving as the footsteps and the crashing came closer. "I can see him," she whispered.

Chris sat up in his sleeping bag. "What's going on?" Laura saw one or two other heads rise.

"Start yelling," Irene told Brian. "I won't ask again."

"You guys get outa here!" Brian shouted. At the same time Laura heard footsteps from the opposite side of camp. She turned unbelievingly. Wally came running toward them. He looked at Brian, who was still shouting, and hesitated for a second. Then he bent over and grabbed up one of the sleeping bags.

Several people screamed, and Laura was surprised to find herself running toward him. She jumped over somebody who was crawling out of a sleeping bag and followed Wally as he threw his bundle over his shoulder and ran back toward the tents.

Racing forward, Laura could see the bag shaking and twisting. She grabbed a corner of the bag and pulled. The sudden yank caused Wally to trip and step sideways to keep from falling. He turned to face her, his body dropping into a crouch. When he saw Laura, still pulling on the bag, he merely shoved her backward with his free hand and tramped off into the darkness.

"It's John," Donna shouted. "He's got John."

Laura pulled herself to her feet and turned back toward the fire. "Irene?"

"Don't worry, honey. I didn't hurt him. He couldn't

have stopped that big moose any more than you could. Did he hurt you?"

"No," Laura said quickly.

"Laura," Donna said, running toward her, "he's got John." She threw her arms around Laura and sobbed. Stephanie was quickly beside them. Laura hugged both girls tightly.

"Everybody settle down," Irene said. "We'll make it all right."

"What'll we do now?" Donna sobbed.

"I'll tell you what," Brian said, grinning up at them. "I think you people got problems."

VI

Laura stared into the darkness, wondering how far into the trees Wally had gone. Irene moved up beside her and spoke into her ear. "Looks like we're gonna have to start the talking."

"Should I go ahead?"

"I think you better. That big guy might start in on John just for the fun of it. Just let me get back over by our buddy there before you start."

"Hey, Wally," Laura shouted. "Wally."

"Yeah?" His voice showed that he was closer than she would have figured.

"If you'll let John go, we'll do the same for Brian."

Brian started to yell something, but Irene smothered it with her hand.

"You let Brian go first," Wally said. He didn't sound very convinced.

"Come on, Wally. We're not that dumb. No tricks. You come here with John, put him down, and take Brian."

There was a long silence, and Laura listened intently

for any movement in the brush. "Hey, Myron," Wally finally yelled, "you over there?"

"Yeah," Myron said. Laura whirled around, expecting from the nearness of his voice to be able to see him. She could see only the outline of trees, but Myron had to be somewhere among them.

"You want Louie and me to try to jump that other guy?" Chris whispered to Laura.

"Not while Wally has John," Laura said.

"I guess you're right." Chris moved back toward the fire.

"Myron," Wally called, "should I do it?"

"Heck, yes," Myron shouted. "Let's get going."

"Listen, Wally," Laura said quickly. "We'll put Brian over by the tents, and then we'll move back. You come in and set John down and pick up Brian. You can carry Brian, can't you?"

"Yeah, I can carry him."

"All right. We're moving Brian over there right now." She turned back to the campfire. "Chris, Louie, give me a hand."

"I had to tape his mouth," Irene said. "He was going to be a problem."

Brian's eyes glared at Irene. His lips moved beneath the tape, but Laura could not tell what he was saying.

"I'll get him under the arms," Chris said. "You two get his legs." The three of them hauled Brian across the clearing, stopping only once to rest. Beverly walked along beside them, looking down at Brian.

"Where do you want him?" Louie asked.

"This is far enough, I think," Laura said. "Let's put him down." It was a relief to let go of him. "Brian," she said, keeping her voice friendly, "you're heavier than you look."

Beverly knelt down beside Brian and brushed some dirt from his hair. "Brian," she said quietly, "please go back and leave us alone. I know you're mad right now, but please let it go. Okay?" She bent over and pressed her lips against his forehead, then followed Chris and Louie back to the fire.

Laura waited until the others had moved away, then spoke quietly. "I'm sorry, Brian. I'm sorry this whole thing got started. We didn't mean for things to work out like this, and I'm sure you didn't either. Now I'm begging you. Please forgive us for what we've done. Please forget the whole thing. This is one of those nightmares that we all need to end. And you're the only one that can do it. Before anybody gets really hurt, please let it go."

Brian jerked his head and moved his mouth beneath the tape. Laura looked back at her group and then called out into the darkness, "Okay, Wally. He's ready whenever you are." She crouched beside Brian. "I'll take off this tape if you'll promise not to yell. Promise?"

Brian stared at her with the coldest eyes she had ever seen. She looked down to avoid them. "If you promise not to yell, just nod your head." He continued to stare, and his head remained rigid. "I know you're mad and hurt. But please don't keep this going. We were scared of you from the beginning, and we're still scared. What we did, we did because we were afraid—not because we wanted to hurt you. Please forgive us. Please write me off as a dumb girl that didn't know any better. And don't keep this going. Please." She looked into his eyes and tried to find something softer and warmer behind the cold stare.

"Here I come," Wally yelled.

"Please, Brian," Laura said. "You don't want to waste your time with us." She stood up quickly and moved back to where the others were standing.

Wally marched into the light, looking around as he walked. He still had the sleeping bag slung over the same shoulder, and Laura wondered if he had carried it the whole time. Wally set down the bag and reached for Brian. John's head and shoulders emerged from the bag, then disappeared as Wally aimed a kick in that direction. The bag began to roll away. Wally hoisted Brian to his shoulder but could not seem to find a balancing point. He quickly changed positions and carried Brian straight in front of him like a load of firewood.

Once Wally had his load arranged, he moved toward the fire. When he reached the rolling sleeping bag, he drove a foot into the middle of it. The whole group winced, as if each one felt the kick. Then Wally stepped over the bag and walked across the clearing, passing a few feet from the fire. He hardly seemed to notice the others as they moved back. He disappeared into the darkness, walking toward the spot where Brian had left his motorcycle.

John crawled out of his sleeping bag, shaking his head. "Wow," he said. The others ran toward him, and he reached out his arms and tried to hug all of them at once.

Irene moved beside him. "Are you all in one piece? Where'd he kick you?"

"He mostly got my arm," John said. "I was all hunched up in there."

He held out his arm, and Irene took his wrist and moved it around. "That doesn't hurt?"

"No, it just hurts where he kicked it." He rolled up his sleeve to show a deep red lump.

"That's nasty, and it's going to hurt for a while," Irene said as she looked it over. "But it's going to be all right, I think. I figure what you need right now is the kind of first aid these girls can give you. A little hugging beats aspirin every time."

"Now you're talking," John said.

The others crowded around him once again. "Were you asleep when he grabbed you?" Donna asked him, patting his neck.

"I didn't even know what was happening. I felt somebody picking me up and hugging me, and I figured it was Beverly."

The motorcycle engine growled and then came to life, roaring and whining. The headlight beamed across the darkness, as the engine was put into gear. Then the light came racing toward them. "Get back," Laura shouted. "Get into the trees."

The motorcycle came bouncing into the circle and headed for one of the running figures. Laura stood helplessly as the cycle roared straight for Donna. Donna looked over her shoulder, her eyes flashing in the light. Just as the cycle seemed about to overtake her, she dived sideways onto the ground, hitting on her shoulders, and rolled over and over.

Brian dug his heel into the earth and spun the rear wheel of the cycle around, spraying dirt into the brush. He turned toward Donna again, but she was up and running once more. When she disappeared into the trees, Brian moved across the now-empty clearing and drove straight into one of the tents. For a minute the engine began to sputter, but then he moved forward again, bringing the tent with him. He spun the rear wheel once more and dragged the tent toward the fire.

He maneuvered the cycle to one side of the fire pit and pulled the tent into the flames. He abandoned the tent and circled the clearing again, deliberately running over as much equipment as possible. He methodically ran over each tent, sometimes circling to take a second run if he was not satisfied with the first assault.

When Chris moved back into the clearing, Brian headed straight for him. Chris stood like a matador for a minute, balanced on the balls of his feet. But Brian slowed, ready to follow any jump. Chris turned and ran back toward the trees with the cycle in pursuit. When Chris leaped behind a stand of trees, Brian laughed and flipped his rear wheel to spray dirt into the area.

Laura stood peering between two pine trees, waiting and watching. The air was heavy with dust and exhaust smoke. The first tent seemed to be smothering the fire, so the only light came from the bouncing headlight of the cycle. Brian was now riding around and around in a tight circle where the sleeping bags had been. From where she stood, Laura could not tell if the bags were still there. She guessed that they were. Otherwise, Brian would not have been so concerned with that spot.

Then he began riding in wider and wider circles, running over everything in his path. A backpack, apparently filled with something solid, caused his front wheel to leap sideways, but he managed to keep the cycle upright.

"Hey, Laura," Louie said, dashing over to where she stood. "You think we ought to go after him?"

"No," Laura said. "Just let him be. As long as nobody's in danger, just let him be. He'll get tired of this sooner or later."

"Oh, man," Louie said, "I rented my stuff from the Sports Lodge. I hope they got insurance."

"Can you tell what he's doing?"

Brian was moving very slowly now, heading toward the fire. He pulled the tent away from the fire pit and began to dump things into the coals. "It's a backpack," Louie said. "He's emptying it into the fire."

"Hey," Brian yelled over the sound of his motor, "where'd everybody go? Look at this stuff. Don't anybody want it?" He suddenly dropped the pack and made a quick circle of the clearing. Nobody had appeared, although Laura saw several pairs of eyes reflecting light. Everybody was doing just as she was, standing behind trees and waiting.

There was another slow trip to the fire and then a third. That time, Brian sat and shouted out the contents. "Here's a bunch of soup. Anybody want it?" He tossed the packet into the fire. "Some oatmeal, too. Forget it." They went into the fire also. "More soup. Who needs it? Here's some cookies. That's more like it." He stuffed several into his mouth. "Anybody want a cookie?" He laughed and stuck the box inside his shirt. "I guess not. Look at this. Somebody's shirt." He held it up and waved it around. Then he took it in both hands and ripped it. "No good now. It's torn. Might as well throw it away." He tossed it onto the fire. Suddenly he dropped the pack and made another circle of the clearing. "Where'd everybody go? You all asleep out there?"

Laura cupped her hand over her watch and peered in to read the luminous dial. It was almost three o'clock. Surely he would tire of this. If they could just wait and let his anger work itself out, he would leave.

Brian made several wide, slow circles, stopping once

to pick up something and throw it away again. He paused by the fire to get some more cookies from the box that he had tucked inside his shirt. "Hey, Beverly, you little fox," he yelled. "Come here and I'll give you a cookie. Just as long as you keep your ignorant mouth shut." He laughed and made another slow circle. "Where'd you go, Beverly?"

On his next circle he stopped for a long time, and Laura could not see what he was doing. "This pack fits pretty good," he shouted. "It's a whole lot better than the thing I got. I think I'll just keep it. You guys don't want it, do ya?" He moved along, stopping once to let his light shine into a clump of trees. "Who's back there? Is that brainless Beverly back there? Come on. Who is it?" He laughed and started forward.

When he reached the fire, he stopped and kicked something toward the middle of the coals. "I'm gonna go now. All of you have a nice sleep, hear? Maybe I'll send Wally over after a while to see how you're doing. He likes you people, especially that little half-pint. And just so you don't get lonely, I'll come back and visit you first thing in the morning. Bye-bye." He turned the motorcycle toward the path and headed away from camp. When he was just beyond the clearing, he slowed, and Laura thought he was going to turn and come back. "Sleep tight, kiddies," he yelled, then raced forward. Laura stood and watched the headlight move away.

"I wonder if it was my pack he got," Louie said.

"All right," Laura shouted. "Let's see what we've got left. Who's got a flashlight?"

Once the first anger and shock were past, Laura realized that the gear was less damaged than she had thought. The tents and sleeping bags were dirty, of course, and several had been torn. But nothing was hopelessly ruined except a shirt of Stephanie's and a little food. Donna's backpack was gone, but nothing else seemed to be missing.

"Thank heaven that tent put out most of the fire," Laura said as she raked packets of dried food out of the ashes. "Most of these things look all right—even if they're scorched a little."

When nobody responded, she turned away from the equipment and supplies. The gear, she suddenly realized, was in better condition than her crew. They stood around the fire, looking into the flames. Donna was crying, and Beverly had her face turned away. "Hey," Laura said, "come on now. It's all right. Everybody's safe, and we're going to get out of here. You'll have to put up with a little extra dirt, but we're okay." They continued to stare at the fire.

"You got a really neat boyfriend, Beverly," Louie said.

"It's not my . . ." Beverly began, but then she began to cry. "I didn't know . . ."

"Yes, you *did*," Amy said. "Anybody could see right away what a creep he was. You just wanted to show what hot stuff you were."

"Leave me alone," Beverly said.

"No use feeling sorry now, Bev," Donna said. "The damage is already done."

"Ease off now," Laura said. "We don't need that."

"You're a fine bunch," Irene shouted. "The whole fat lot of you. You're all so tough now—picking on her. If you wanted a fight, you had plenty of chances to-night. Where were you when that ape was running around here? I didn't see any of you spoiling for a fight then. So you better not start in now."

"We didn't mean anything," Louie said. "We're just tired."

"What do you want to do?" Irene yelled at him. "You want to go to sleep and have a nice nap till he comes back to push you around some more? For heaven's sake, you can't just roll over and play dead. That squirrel had too much fun just now. There he was with a built-in audience, and he was loving every minute of it. So we can fight each other and moan and sleep, or we can get ready for him when he comes back. And you better believe he'll be back."

"But . . ." Amy started.

"Shut up, girl," Irene said. "I don't have enough left in me to argue. Look, forget about tonight. This whole outfit just took it like a bunch of sheep, but that's history now. Next time it's going to be different. As soon as we finish here, I want you to look in your packs for socks—the heavier the better. Get a sock and go down to the lake and fill it up with about four big handfuls of sand. Like this." She reached behind her and drew out a gray sock, knotted at the top and filled almost to the heel. "Hold it right here," she said, closing her hand around the top, "and you've got a blackjack. You don't have to swing it hard. Just quick and solid. And aim for about here." She patted an area on the back of her head. "There are nine of us and three of them. If we stay together, they can't do a thing. If they come after us, we let them get in the middle. Then pop goes the weasel." She brought the sock down onto the palm of her other hand.

"Now you're talking," Louie said.

After stuffing the sock into her belt, Irene reached behind her and picked up a long, straight stick. "And get one of these. Six feet is about right. It doesn't have to be a big heavy thing. You don't hit with it— you poke. Poke and jab." She held her stick in front of her. "Get your hands tight and then poke this way." She made several quick jabs in front of her, then stopped suddenly. The stick fell from her hands. When she spoke again, her voice was a husky whisper. "Keep it moving fast, and nobody can get near you."

"I wish I'd had one of these earlier tonight," John said.

"We were dumb," Chris said. "We should have been ready for them the first time."

"Well, get ready now," Irene said, her voice trembling. "As soon as you get your sock full of sand and find a good stick, come on back and get some rest. One of you may have to carry me outa here in the morning."

Across the lake a motorcycle roared, and a single beam of light played on the trees. Then the engine noise changed pitch, and the light began to move.

"Oh, no!" Amy shouted.

"He's coming back," Donna moaned.

"Maybe he wants to return your pack," John said. He began pawing through the firewood. "Don't worry. This time we'll be waiting for him."

"Go ahead and get your sticks," Irene said. "You got a few minutes, and you might as well make use of them."

"Irene," Laura said, moving her away from where the boys were handing out branches, "are you all right?"

"Honey, I'm just out of gas. Look at that hand." She held out a shaking hand for Laura to see. "I can't hold it any steadier than that. You keep after the kids. They need all the help they can get right now. I don't know if socks full of sand and long sticks are going to do any good, but anything is better than giving up and letting it happen to you. And that's about where they were." Irene's lower jaw was quivering, and she seemed to have trouble getting her mouth to form the words.

"Go rest awhile," Laura said. "We're going to need your help later."

"I'll do that. I just hope you don't need much help,

that's all." She moved over to the fire, sat on the ground, then laid her head against a log.

Laura moved far enough up the slope so that she could follow the headlight of the motorcycle. It bounced along slowly, following the trail beside the lake. In another hundred yards it would reach the junction where the path to their camp met the main trail. As soon as the cycle turned onto the path, she would gather all of them together. She turned and glanced behind her. There were several flashlights at the creek and one or two at the woodpile. Irene lay in the same position.

The motorcycle continued to move along the trail. Its pace seemed slow, almost leisurely. The motor did little more than hum. Laura held onto a tree and waited for the cycle to turn toward her. She couldn't tell, in the darkness, exactly where the junction was, but it had to be soon. The motorcycle continued to move along, keeping the same even speed.

Even when the cycle had clearly gone beyond the path, Laura remained uncertain. Perhaps he had missed the path and would turn and retrace his way. The headlight grew harder to spot, little flashes of light visible through the trees. The engine sounds grew softer and softer. Still, Laura waited, maintaining her grip on the tree.

When she could no longer spot the headlight, she moved back down the slope. The others were standing by the fire, sticks in hand. "He's gone on," she told them. "I don't know what that means, but at least he's not coming here."

"We'd better keep watch," Chris said, waving his branch.

"One of us at a time," Laura said. "We need to get as rested as possible. We only have a couple of hours until daylight, but even a little sleep would help. Get your sleeping bags and make use of your time."

In two minutes the sleeping bags were once more arranged in a tight circle, and everyone but Chris and Laura was inside. Irene was asleep beside the log, and Laura had wrapped a bag around her without waking her.

"I'll keep watch," Chris whispered. "I haven't done much up to now."

"Thank you, Chris. I really could use the rest." She slipped off her shoes and crawled into her sleeping bag. "Wake somebody when you start getting sleepy."

"I'll be all right," Chris said. He continued to stand beside the fire.

Laura lay motionless, feeling the rocks against her hipbone, and listened to the sounds of the night—a frog grinding out its strange song, some crickets, a bird of some kind, a touch of wind through the tops of the pines. She dozed for a time, but a dream about a motorcycle startled her awake. As she lay and tried to make her way back toward sleep, she found herself thinking of the motorcycle.

What had happened to make one of them leave the

others? Could they have argued? Perhaps Myron had had enough. But why not wait until morning? Why set out on that trail in the darkness?

Suddenly Laura was no longer sleepy. The only explanation for the last mortocycle had finally come to her. What she had been too exhausted to realize earlier was suddenly apparent. There was only one reason for a single rider to make that trip along the trail—to keep them from slipping away in the early hours of the morning.

Their escape route, the trail to Jack Pine Lake, was cut off.

VII

Laura rolled onto her back, stared up at the tops of the trees, and wondered vaguely if it was daylight yet. She glanced over at the fire, and Chris, hunched into a ball, waved at her. He stood up slowly, working his arms back and forth, and came over beside Laura. He knelt down and whispered, "Good morning."

"Didn't you get any sleep at all?"

"I wasn't sleepy. Everything's quiet."

"That's good."

"I've been thinking. Maybe I should sneak over there and slash the tires on their cycles or something."

"I don't know, Chris. I think we'd better stick together from now on. Besides, we should be leaving here right away. Thanks for doing guard duty. I really needed the rest."

"It was about time I did something," Chris said.

"Hey, come on."

"I mean it. One punch, and I was out of it. How does that make me look?"

"That's crazy. He's older than you and a lot bigger, and he hit you with a sucker punch. Right?"

"Yeah, but . . ."

"Yeah, but nothing. I'm just glad you're on our side. You say anything back, and *I'll* hit you with a sucker punch."

Chris smiled at her. "You want me to wake the others?"

"I hate to do it, but maybe we'd better. Keep it quiet, though. I'd like to get out of here without having company."

Everyone seemed to understand the need for speed. The sleeping bags were immediately rolled up. While the others gathered the odds and ends that Brian had scattered around camp, Louie and Amy folded and packed the tents. Chris and John distributed the gear that would have gone into Donna's missing pack. Only Irene seemed lost, wandering back and forth without any apparent purpose.

When everybody sat around the fire for a breakfast of dried apricots and granola bars, there was still only a rosy glow in the eastern sky. "Okay," Laura said, setting down her plate, "remember the motorcycle that we thought was coming here last night? Whoever that was has the trail to Jack Pine cut off. They think they have us trapped, but we're going to fool them. We're going to climb the rockslide over there. It's rough going, but people do it all the time. Cold Springs Lake

is on the other side of the ridge, and some people go
up the slide rather than hike all the way around by
the trail. Those guys may see us, of course, but there's
no way they can follow us on their motorcycles."

"But then what?" Chris asked her. "How do we
get back from there?" He stood up, his stick in his
right hand.

"Two choices. We can either spend a day or so at
Cold Springs Lake and then come back this way, or
we can hike on out to another trailhead—Baker
Meadows—and get somebody to drive us back to pick
up our cars. That's probably the best idea."

"Why don't we just go out the way we came in?"
Chris asked, looking down at Stephanie. "Right now,
I mean. I can't see getting chased off like a bunch of
rabbits. If there's a guy out there on the trail, so what?
There are nine of us."

"Let's go up the slide," Amy said. "We can make it."

"Sure we can," Laura said.

Chris shook his head. "I don't know. That looks like
a rough way to go. We make that climb, and then
we're still nowhere. Why don't we just go back the
way we came? I can't see nine people getting chased
off by three bums. I can just see hiking out to that
other place—what'd you say, Baker Meadows?—and
telling somebody there that three guys chased us off."

Several people nodded. "We can make it," John said.

"If we go up the slide," Laura insisted, "we know that
we won't have motorcycles on our tails."

"I think we've been pushed around enough," Chris said, "and there's only one guy out there. What does everybody else think? Everybody that thinks we ought to go back the way we came, raise your hand."

Laura started to speak and then stopped as the hands began to rise. Irene's hand was up immediately, and the others followed. Only Laura and Amy kept their hands down.

Laura decided not to argue. "All right," she said quickly, "we'll give it a try. Fill up your canteens and water bottles. We'll go in five minutes."

"Let's move it," Chris said.

Laura turned away from the others and grabbed two empty pots. She filled them with lake water and returned to douse the fire. Irene sat in the same spot, staring at the coals. Even as Laura drowned the fire, Irene's gaze did not change.

"We'd better get started," Laura said as she packed away the pots.

Irene looked up at her. "I'm sorry, honey. I wasn't trying to go against you. I just didn't think I could make it up that slide."

"We'll see what happens," Laura said.

"I hate to say it, but I think I better give Donna my pack. She's a big, healthy thing. She can carry it all right."

"Sure she can. You take it easy for a while."

"I'm just all in," Irene said, still sitting in the same position.

Laura arranged a pot in Irene's pack and then tied the cords. It was frightening to see Irene that way, exhausted and lifeless. It was hard to believe that the woman who sat huddled by the dead fire was the same one who had overpowered Brian the night before.

When Donna came back, Laura called her off to the side. "I think it would be a good move if you carried Irene's pack for a while."

"Sure," Donna said. "Is she all right? She looks different. Did she get hurt or something?"

"No, she's just worn out."

"I still wouldn't want to tangle with her," Donna said.

It was just after six o'clock when they started. Chris led the way, his stick in his right hand. Laura stood beside the trail and watched the others pass, each carrying a stout branch and each with a sock full of sand hooked onto a belt or a pack. Irene brought up the rear. She had no stick, but there was a sock full of sand looped over her belt.

"I'll be all right, honey," Irene said. "It just takes longer to get my old blood flowing. I'm feeling better."

Laura took a final look across the lake, pleased with the lack of movement in that direction. With any luck at all, her crew would be at Jack Pine Lake by mid-morning. They might even be able to hike out with the couple that had passed by the night before. As she moved away from the camp, Laura stepped away from the trail and picked up a long stick. It felt heavy and awkward in her hand.

They had traveled for about twenty minutes when Laura saw the people ahead of her come to a sudden stop. She made her way around Irene and Louie, thinking of the snake from the day before. In front of her John and Donna turned, their fingers to their lips.

"What is it?" Laura whispered.

"I don't know," Donna said. "That guy, I guess."

Laura stepped past Donna and followed John forward to where Stephanie and Amy were crouched beside a stand of buckbrush. The others came right behind her. "Chris went up ahead," Stephanie whispered.

Chris crept back toward them, saying nothing until he was beside them. "It's the fat one—Wally," he whispered. "He's asleep in the middle of the trail."

"Is there any way we can slip around him?" Laura asked.

"I don't think so. He picked a rough spot. It's pretty much straight up and down—one of those places where the trail's been chipped out of the rock. I can't see any other way to go."

"All right," Laura said quickly. "Let's head back to the slide. We haven't lost much time."

"No," Chris said. "It's still nine to one. I don't care how big that elephant is. If we go right ahead, there's nothing he can do. All we have to do is show him we aren't scared, and we'll handle him all right."

"I think we should go back," Laura said. "There's no telling what he'll do. It doesn't make sense to take a chance."

"Sometimes you've got to take a chance," Chris said. "Louie? John? You guys are with me, right?"

"Sure," John said.

"I guess so," Louie answered.

"We'll go first, but we need everybody right with us. He's got to see nothing but sticks coming after him. Let's go before he hears anything." Chris moved forward slowly, his stick held out in front of him. The rest followed. "Keep it moving," he whispered.

Laura sighed as she fell in with the others. Thirty feet ahead of them Wally was in his sleeping bag, lying sideways across the trail. Just beyond where he lay, his motorcycle leaned against the bank. Two separate fantasies came to Laura at once. One was that they could simply creep past him, stepping over his huge body and going on. The other was that they could tie him where he lay, the way the little people had handled Gulliver.

Chris kept moving forward, his stick bobbing up and down with each deliberate step. Louie and John followed him, a half step back on either side. The rest bunched together behind the three. Laura kept pressing toward the front until she was walking directly behind Chris.

Wally slowly turned onto his back. He brought one hand out of the bag, rubbed something behind his ear, and let the hand fall once more.

Chris was about fifteen feet away by then, and he had slowed almost to a stop. Laura wondered if Chris was trying to be quiet or trying to decide what to do. She felt strangely removed from what was happening, as if she were watching it on television.

Wally's head jerked up, and he looked directly away from them, toward his motorcycle. Chris moved forward quickly. Wally scratched his ear and slowly turned his head toward them. Chris raised his stick higher as he continued to walk forward.

"Aaaaaah," Wally screamed when he saw them. He began a scrambling crawl, which freed him from the sleeping bag. He continued to crawl for several more feet before he managed to pull himself upright. Chris and the rest moved forward steadily, but they did not try to keep up with Wally, who at first ran and then turned and began to back away.

Laura felt as if she were watching from a long distance away. She saw that Wally had his shoes on. That was odd. But as they marched past his sleeping bag, she saw that it had not been zipped. Apparently Wally had just wrapped the bag around himself for warmth. It made no difference, of course, but nevertheless, Laura was glad to have the puzzle solved.

"Get out of here," Wally yelled at them. "You get out of here."

Wally's shouts seemed to revive everyone. The pace quickened, and the group moved forward, past the motorcycle, their sticks bouncing. Wally kept backing up, occasionally taking glances over his shoulder as if he expected someone to appear from that direction.

As Laura moved forward with the others, the reality of the situation descended upon her. She was no longer watching the events, a remote spectator; she was there. She swallowed twice and called out, "Wally, we're on our way home. We aren't going to cause any trouble. We just want to go home."

Wally continued to back up, moving slowly up the trail. When he reached a particularly steep section of the trail, he turned and climbed it, continuing to glance over his shoulder with each step. "Get out of here," he shouted while he continued to move backward.

"We're on our way home," Laura called. "We aren't going to cause any trouble." She tried to keep her voice soothing and reassuring. "We're on our way home. It's all right, Wally. We're just heading for home."

The procession continued upward, deliberately but without stopping. Wally stayed about twenty feet ahead of them. If they slowed, he did the same. Laura kept speaking, even though she realized that she was talking the same way that she would to a wild animal, relying more on her tone of voice than her words. "It's all right, Wally. We don't want any trouble. We just want to go home."

They had reached a level section of the trail, and Wally had moved a little farther ahead of them. Laura could hear the panting of the people around her. As the trail widened, John and Louie moved up beside Chris, and Laura suddenly had someone on each side of her. "Just let us go on by, Wally," she began again. "We don't want any trouble. We're on our way home."

"Get out of here," Wally yelled. "Get out." As he began to shout, he stopped moving backward. He stared at them and lowered his head. "Get out of here."

"Get ready," Chris muttered. "He's coming. Don't step back, whatever you do."

"Get out!" Wally roared. He ran toward them, his head down and his hands out in front of him, as if they were about to grab something.

As Wally rushed toward them, Laura steadied her hands on her branch. The boys in front of her crouched down, keeping their sticks directly in front of them, aimed in the direction of Wally's chest. Donna moved next to Laura, leveling her stick with the others.

Wally's steps began to slow as he came closer to them. What had begun as a charge had shifted to a jog. He kept looking at them as he came forward, as if he expected them to do something. When he was a few steps in front of the sticks, he stopped abruptly and shouted, "Get back!"

"Move up," Chris said. "Move up." He took a step

toward Wally, and the others followed. Wally shuffled backward. "Faster," Chris said. Wally turned away and ran back up the trail.

"Attaway," John shouted.

"Charge!" Louie yelled.

"Just keep moving," Chris said. "As long as we stay together, we're all right."

Wally stopped twenty feet ahead of them. "You get out of here," he bellowed.

"We just want to go home," Laura called. "We're on our way home."

Once more the procession began, although everyone was moving faster now. Wally stayed a few feet farther ahead, but he continued to walk backward except when he came to a steep section.

"This is like a cattle drive," Louie said. "Except we have just one big ox."

"Why doesn't he just get out of the way?" Amy said.

"Let's forget it, Wally," Laura called. "There's no problem. We just want to go home, and that's what we're going to do."

"Maybe we could tell him to stop and let us have a break," Louie said. "He wouldn't mind if we had a little water, would he?"

"Keep moving," Chris said. "And keep your eyes open. He might try to charge us anytime."

As they moved closer to the top of the ridge, the trail grew steeper and narrower. Chris and Louie went ahead, with John and Donna directly behind them. Wally kept moving backward through a series of switchbacks. Laura kept watching Wally and wondering what was going through his mind. At times, when the trail cut back upon itself, he would be just above the last of their group so that someone could have reached out with a long pole and tapped his foot. But Wally paid no attention to what lay below him. He kept watching Chris and Louie.

Wally was walking sideways, keeping his eyes on the group, when he came to a division in the trail. The main trail was a long switchback, but hikers had created a shortcut by moving straight downhill and avoiding the long loop. Wally stopped short and stared down the trail at them.

Laura could see the problem Wally faced. If he stayed on the main path, someone might possibly scramble up the shortcut and get ahead of him. But if he went up the shortcut, someone might be able to race around the loop and beat him to the top. Wally stood with his back to the two trails and watched them advance.

"Get back," he shouted. "Get out of here."

Chris and Louie moved forward steadily, closing the distance between Wally and themselves. Wally turned and scrambled up the steep shortcut, using his hands to pull himself forward. When he had reached a flat spot, he turned and looked behind him, as if he expected to see the others at his heels.

Chris and Louie had stopped. Wally's scramble up the shortcut had sent a wake of rocks and dirt crashing down behind him, and Chris had moved back to avoid these. When Wally saw them standing motionless, he laughed and began kicking more rocks, sending them crashing onto the trail. The group edged backward.

"Get out of here," Wally shouted. He used his boots to send down another stream of rocks. "Get out of here."

Then he began to grab up rocks and throw them. His throws were erratic, and he seemed not to be aiming at all.

"Look out!" someone screamed as rocks began to land on all sides. Laura felt herself being pushed against the bank as people raced past her.

For a moment there was only panic as all of them dashed down the trail. Then Beverly screamed and plunged forward into the dirt, her pack rattling and clanging as she hit the ground and slid to a stop. Laura ran down the trail toward her.

Beverly lay struggling in the dust, trying to reach her feet again. Laura seized her arm and held it tightly. "I'll help you, Bev."

Beverly pulled against her. "Don't hold me back!" she screamed, trying to crawl forward. "Let go of me!"

Laura kept hold of the arm and raised Beverly to her knees. "Try to stand up, Bev." Beverly's face and hair were covered with blood and dust, and Laura couldn't tell where the wound was. "Come on. You can make it."

"Hurry," Beverly said, scrambling to her feet. She lunged ahead, pulling Laura along with her. Somewhere behind them a rock hit and bounced.

Then Irene was on the other side, and the two of them were holding Beverly upright. After the first frantic steps Beverly seemed to have lost control of her legs. "I'm dying," she said, sobbing. "I'm dying."

Laura stared at the trail ahead of her, afraid that she would be sick if she looked over at Beverly. "You'll be all right, kiddo," Irene said, her voice calm and reassuring. "I know it hurts right now, but you'll be fine. It's a cut on your scalp, and it hurts like crazy and bleeds a lot, but it heals quick and won't even leave a scar."

"You can make it, Bev," Laura said, still not looking at her.

Chris came running toward them. "Right down here," he said. "There's a bunch of trees. We'll be okay there." He stopped and began backing up as they continued toward him. "What can I do to help?"

"If it's not too far, just get out of the way," Irene said. "Where are we headed?"

"Just to where the trail bends. The others are right by those trees."

"Get Donna's pack open and get some water ready," Irene told him.

Laura stumbled along, using both of her hands to keep Beverly upright. "Come on, Bev," she said. "Just a little ways farther. Just a few more steps." A rock struck above them and bounced over their heads, hitting the ground somewhere below. Beverly moaned.

At the bend in the trail Louie and John came and took Beverly, stripped off her pack, and helped her sit down. Irene knelt beside her and began to work on the wound. "It's all right, sweetheart," she said, swabbing the area. "It'll heal without a scar. You just wait."

While the rest gathered around Beverly, Laura unbuckled her pack and collapsed on the ground. "Are you all right, Laura?" Irene called to her.

"I will be in a minute."

"If you start to get dizzy, get your head between your legs."

"I'm okay." For a minute she sat with her eyes shut and allowed her muscles to relax. Her breathing gradually slowed until she could once more breathe through her nose.

When she opened her eyes, Stephanie was kneeling beside her. "Did you get hit, Laura?"

"No. Do I look like it?"

"Sort of."

Laura looked down at her hands, which were sticky with drying blood. She unbuckled her canteen, took a sip, and then began to wash off her hands. "It's probably a waste of water," she said, "but it makes me feel better."

Hearing scuffling behind her, Laura turned to see Chris, Louie, and John running back up the trail. Each was carrying a handful of rocks. As they moved farther up the hill, rocks began to land around them, hitting and bouncing on out of sight. The boys stopped, threw a few of their own rocks, then raced back to the trees. Rocks continued to come from above, one or two striking the upper limbs of the trees where the others were sitting.

"I almost got him," Louie shouted. "I hit up above him, and a bunch of junk came down right by him."

"Can't get any force throwing uphill," John said. "I'd like to get up above him for two minutes. Then we'd see how he looked."

"Let's give it another try," Chris said. "We may get off a lucky throw this time."

A rock landed next to the tree and bounced down the hill. "Move back some more," Laura shouted. Another rock struck a branch and came rattling down beside her.

"We'd better get out there," Chris yelled. "Maybe we can chase him back a ways."

"Chris!" Laura shouted. "Don't go out there again."

Chris turned and looked at her. "Hey, we gotta do something."

"I know," Laura said, "but not that. This is crazy. We've got one person hurt already." She moved up beside Chris. "Look at Bev over there. Look carefully. That's what this is all about. And that could be a skull fracture for all we know. Or the next one could be."

"Yeah, but we can't just—"

"Stick with me, Chris. There's got to be another way." She stepped away from the tree just as another rock landed on the trail in front of her. "Wally!" she shouted. "Hey, Wally!"

"Whatcha want?"

Laura was relieved that he was still some distance to her right. "Beverly's been hurt. We need to get her out of here right away."

There was a long silence, and Laura hoped that he was not creeping in her direction. "It's not my fault," he shouted finally. He hadn't moved. "I told you to get back."

"It doesn't matter whose fault it is. What matters is that we get her out of here. I want you to let us go by."

"No," he yelled. "I told you to get back, and you better do it."

"Wally, we have to get Beverly to a doctor. We don't know how badly she's hurt."

"It's not my fault. I told you." Laura could hear the anxiety in his voice. "You made me do it."

"You're right, Wally. It's not your fault. Nobody wants to blame you. We just need to get her to a doctor."

"It's not my fault. I told you to get back."

"We need to get her out of here. I want you to let us go by."

"Get back," Wally yelled. A rock landed some distance in front of Laura.

"Wally, we just want to go away and leave you alone."

"Get back," he shouted again. Laura felt her body tense as she waited for another rock to land, but nothing happened.

"All right," she shouted. "We'll do it. We'll go back."

"Yeah?" Wally said after a minute.

"But we're afraid you'll throw rocks at us. Will you promise not to throw any rocks if we go back the way we came and leave you alone?"

There was a long silence, and Laura listened for movement. "Get out of here," Wally shouted. It was hard to tell whether or not he was closer.

"Will you promise not to throw rocks?"

"Just hurry up," Wally yelled. "Hurry up and get out."

"We can hurry if you promise not to throw rocks."

"Get going."

It was clear to Laura that he was not going to say the words. "All right," she called. "We'll go in just a minute." She turned and headed back to the trees. "Get your packs on," she said. "I think we'll be safe if we go right now."

"You mean back the way we came?" Chris asked unhappily.

"It's the only direction open right now," Laura said.

Amy had her pack on and was helping Donna. "Let's go," she said. "There's nothing to stay here for."

Irene was sitting beside Beverly, both of them leaning against a tree trunk. There was a small bandage on
Beverly's forehead, just below the hairline. Her clothes
were covered with blood, and her face was still streaked
with reddish lines, but Laura was astounded at how
much better she looked.

"You look great, Bev. How you feeling?"

"I'm still kind of shaky."

"I don't blame you. I feel the same way, and I
didn't even get hit."

"She got first-rate care," Irene said, reaching over
and patting Beverly's hand. "I put a butterfly bandage
on there that would make a plastic surgeon jealous.
This time next week she won't be able to find it."

"Do you think you can walk?" Laura asked Beverly.

"She can outrun me," Irene said.

"What about you, Irene? Can you handle a pack for
a while?"

"I'll be all right on the downhill run," Irene said.
"Come on, Beverly. We're going to take you back to
the creek and wash off that pretty face of yours." She
stood up and maneuvered herself into Beverly's pack.
She squirmed and shifted until Louie came and helped
her make some adjustments. Beverly got to her feet
and held onto the tree.

"Can you make it, Bev?" Laura asked.

"Let's go," Beverly said quietly. "I just want to get
somewhere so I can clean up." Her first steps were
shaky, but she kept moving.

Irene buckled her hip belt. "She'll make it. She's a tough kid, and she's had the best medical care in the state."

As Laura followed the others down the trail, she kept an eye on Wally. He moved downhill also, keeping about fifty yards between himself and them. Although he carried a rock in each hand, he seemed peaceful enough until the group approached his motorcycle.

Then he charged toward them, yelling, "You better not touch it. You touch it, and I'll kill you."

Laura watched him race toward them as she called out, "We won't touch your motorcycle. We promise. We won't touch it."

Wally slowed his pace as he came near Laura. "You better not touch it," he shouted.

"We won't," Laura said, moving forward quickly. "See? We're going right on by. We wouldn't put a finger on it." She walked past the motorcycle, staying as far away as the trail would allow. Behind her she could hear Wally's clumping footsteps. When the footsteps stopped abruptly, she hurried forward, expecting at any moment to hear the cycle. When she finally glanced back, she saw Wally sitting in the trail, pulling his sleeping bag around himself.

Laura turned and, for the first time that day, looked across at French Lake and the rockslide that awaited them. Even from that distance the slide looked enormous.

VIII

As she walked past the campsite, Laura was glad to be bringing up the rear. She couldn't have hidden the discouragement and frustration she felt at being back where they started, and it was a relief not to have to try. So much time and energy spent—and nothing accomplished.

Across the lake somebody was standing at the shore-line, looking in their direction. Laura took a deep breath and let the air go. She hadn't dared hope for much, but she *had* thought that Brian might still be asleep.

"Look at that gorgeous water," she shouted as her crew plodded down toward the creek. If she was frightened and discouraged—and there was no denying she was—the rest must be feeling the same. And they would be looking to her. She didn't have much to offer them at that point—no miracles, no clever schemes, not even much energy. But at least she wouldn't weigh them down with her own misgivings. "Wash your faces and get your canteens full," she called. "There's no more water until we get over the ridge."

The stay at the creek seemed interminable to Laura. She tried to hurry the others, but she didn't want anyone to panic. Once she had filled her canteen and washed the dried blood from her arms, she stepped across the stream and walked to the top of the opposite bank. She had never been past the creek, and she wasn't sure what lay before them.

The path, as nearly as she could tell, followed the shoreline, although some distance above it. There was another campsite or two on that side of the creek, but from there on, the path dwindled. Only an occasional fisherman or hiker would circle the lake that way. With the slide at the west end of the lake, it was much faster to head in the opposite direction.

"Let's get moving," Amy said. "What are we waiting for?"

But there were several delays. Beverly had to change her clothes, Donna's pack had to be adjusted, and somebody needed a Band-Aid after all.

Laura paced back and forth, gritted her teeth, and tried to keep smiling. "Time's up," she finally shouted. "Let's get moving." She slipped into her pack and climbed the bank once again. "Get your packs on, and let's go." She headed away from them, hoping to hurry them along.

As she moved away from the rushing water of the

creek, she could hear the motorcycles. It took all of her strength to keep from screaming. Her view was blocked by the trees that surrounded her, but she knew that they were coming.

"Oh, no!" Amy shouted, running toward Laura. "What are we going to do?"

"We're going to keep moving. Will you lead out?"

"All right." Amy headed away at a pace that was little short of a trot.

"Hurry it up," Laura called. "The motorcycles are coming. If we move right along, we should be up the rockslide before they ever get here."

As she hurried along at the end of the line, Laura found it difficult to tell whether the cycles were getting closer. With her group clumping through the brush and with so many echoes, she could not be sure of anything.

When Brian suddenly appeared on the trail behind her, Laura was more surprised than she should have been. The engine sounds had not grown any louder, and she had lost some of her apprehension. But then he was there, some twenty yards behind her. "Into the brush," she shouted. "Get into the brush. But stay together and keep moving toward the slide." She dashed off the path, yanking her pack free from a vine. "Stay together and keep moving." But already she could see them scatter, some on one side of the path, some on the other.

Brian accelerated, and his cycle seemed to leap toward Laura. She could not run through the thick brush, but she managed to get far enough so that a motorcycle couldn't follow.

Brian continued up the path, shouting something which Laura could not hear. A few feet behind Brian came Myron, crouched low on his cycle, his eyes almost level with his hands. Laura kept watching the path, but Wally did not appear. She could only wonder whether he was lagging behind or whether he was still up on the main trail.

Ahead of her Brian had left the path and was crashing through the brush, following somebody. Myron slowed and then stopped, still on the path. Laura, remembering her shouted advice, began to move forward. Brian appeared on the path again, laughing and shouting, then moved into the brush on the opposite side. Laura could see Amy and Louie running ahead of him. When they disappeared into a thicket, he circled once, stopped, and then came roaring back to the path.

Laura sensed that she was getting cut off from the others. She was in a dense stand of brush, which she could not penetrate, no matter how she maneuvered. Finally, when the sounds of the motorcycles were farther ahead, she crept back to the path and trotted along, seeking out escape routes that she could take if she saw one of them. She could hear the motorcycle far ahead of her, and she felt reasonably secure as she hurried forward.

Off to her left somebody was still crouching in the

trees. "Come on," she shouted. "Keep moving toward the slide." She peered through the brush, trying to make out who it was. "Come back to the path if you have to. We can go together." As the figure moved, Laura saw that it was Irene. "Come on, Irene. I'll wait for you."

Laura turned back to the path in time to see Myron hurtling toward her. She tried to dive into the brush, but she could not get her legs to move. She had to decide whether to take a step forward or backward in order to move around a clump of manzanita. But she could not seem to make the decision. She shuffled her feet, as if trying to go both ways at once.

Myron headed toward her, his hand groping for the brake pedal. Laura was intensely aware of the horror on his face as the motorcycle bore down on her. She took a step backward, but it was too late to dive. The cycle was almost upon her. She heard herself scream as she backed against the brush.

Then Myron was jamming his foot into the dirt, sending gravel and dust flying as he veered off the path, away from Laura. His elbow brushed against her as he passed. Then he was in the air, flying over the handlebars, as the cycle struck something that would not be moved.

Laura stood for a moment, stunned by the noise and the dirt and the smell of hot oil. She took a few steps toward the slide, then called back, "Are you all right?"

"Yeah, I'm all right." Myron's voice was unsteady, almost a sob.

"Are you sure?"

"Look, will you get outa here? I'm all right. Just hurry up and get away from here, okay?"

"Okay," Laura said. She turned and hurried along the path. She could hear the other engine roaring far ahead of her, so she rushed forward while she could.

Around the first bend a huge log lay across the path. It was here, she was sure, that Myron had turned around. Somehow Brian had continued, although she didn't know how. She climbed over the log quickly, stopping for a moment to listen. Brian was yelling, and the motor was roaring. It was hard to tell whether he was fighting with some of the group or whether he was just amusing himself.

When Brian's noise grew louder, Laura left the path and moved uphill. For a time she moved around the scattered rocks, but that was soon impossible. The last of the brush and trees disappeared, and she found herself on the rockslide. The slide was a mass of rocks —some the size of basketballs, others the size of automobiles. It was several hundred yards across and more yards up than Laura wanted to think about. On either side of this huge rock pile, beginning some distance above the lake, steep cliffs rose, remnants of the mass that had collapsed to form the slide.

It was difficult to move on the rocks. The surfaces were rough, and Laura found it hard to guess which rocks would be stable and which would tip as soon as she put her weight on them. She found herself nudging each rock before she stood on it. It was going to be a long climb.

"Laura," she heard. "Up here."

She looked above her to see Amy waving her hand. There were several others with her. Laura made her way over a huge boulder and slid across the upper side. Her pack pulled on her shoulders as she bent over and picked her way through a field of smaller rocks.

"We didn't know what happened to you," Amy said as Laura climbed toward them.

"I took the scenic route," Laura said.

"Have you seen Irene?"

"Not for a while," Laura said. "We got split up back there."

"Everybody else is here. Should we go back and try to find her?"

"She might be insulted by a rescue party," Laura said. She slipped out of her pack and sat down close to the others. "Let's give her a few minutes."

"Everybody's all right," Amy continued.

"More or less," Beverly said. She was sitting in the shade of a boulder, with her head bent forward.

"We've been looking around," Donna said. "Nobody can find the trail."

"I don't think there is one," Laura said. "I think we have to go this one on our own."

"But what about up there?" Amy asked, pointing above her. "It looks like a cliff at the very top. There must be a trail up there."

"I don't know," Laura said, not bothering to look up. "All I know is that people go from here to Cold Springs Lake. So there has to be a way to do it."

"Maybe we ought to go back after Irene," Chris said.

"Wait a little while," Laura told him. "I figure that she probably found a good safe spot to sit out the action."

"He couldn't touch us," John said. "A motorcycle's no good in brush like that."

"He's just lucky," Louie said. "I was going to thrash him within an inch of his life, but he didn't get in my way." He leaned back and laughed.

"Nobody could have gotten in your way," Amy said. "You passed me up like I was standing still."

"Sure I did," Louie said. "But that's because you were standing there with your thumb out, trying to hitch a ride."

"Irene should be getting here pretty soon," Laura said. She stood up and moved to the top of a rock. Directly below them lay the peaceful blue-green waters of the lake. Off to the left were the manzanita thickets and pine trees that they had come from. Somewhere far off was the sound of the motorcycles, but Laura could not judge the direction.

Chris stood up and moved beside Laura. "I'll go take a look. It's not too bad climbing around these rocks when you don't have a pack on."

"I'd go along," Louie said, "but Beverly and Amy get lonely when I'm gone."

"There's no need for anybody else to go," Chris said.

"Okay, klutzo," Donna said to her brother, "now you can volunteer. You know you won't have to go."

"You go," John said. "If they get close, you can scare 'em away. Just smile at 'em."

"I'll be back in a minute," Chris said. He made his way downhill, cutting a zigzag path through the boulders.

"Everybody sit down and relax," Laura said. "You're going to need all the rest you can get." She leaned against a rock and watched Chris move along.

"The question is," Louie said, "how long do we wait before we send somebody after Chris?"

"Just shut up, Louie," Stephanie said.

Laura kept a careful eye on her watch, knowing the time would seem much longer than it actually was. Ten minutes passed. Then five more. A motorcycle appeared on the far side of the lake, moving slowly. She could not tell whether it was Brian or Myron, and she couldn't guess why one of them would be headed that way.

When Chris and Irene emerged from the brush, Laura felt a wave of relief spill over her. Chris was carrying Irene's pack, but he still had to keep stopping to wait for her. The two of them made their way up the slide slowly. Several times Irene had to retrace her steps, apparently unable to follow Chris over some of the larger boulders.

When the two of them reached the spot where the others were waiting, Chris set down the pack and lay down on the ground. Irene sank onto a rock. "Boy, oh, boy," she said, "this is one old lady that ain't cut out for rock climbing."

"You came right up," Laura said.

"Somebody give me some water," Irene said. "I'm about to die."

Donna, who was closest to Irene, poured water into her tin cup and handed it over. "Is your canteen empty?"

Irene sipped the water slowly. "No," she said between sips, "I haven't touched it. I just didn't have the strength to get it out right now."

"Where'd you two meet?" Laura asked Chris.

"On the trail. She was headed right this way. She just got caught back there and couldn't move."

Irene nodded and sipped again.

"Caught?" Laura asked.

"Not caught, thank heaven," Irene said. "Just cut off. Give me a minute." She tipped up the cup and then handed it back to Donna. "Thanks, hon. You're a lifesaver." She shifted around to face Laura. "You know when that monkey went off the path and took a spill?"

"Yeah. He swerved to miss me."

"Well, he came darn close to hitting me. I was just on the other side of some brush, and I didn't dare move. So there I was, and there I had to stay. And then that other one—that Brian—came along. There was something bent on that first guy's bike, and they spent a while fooling with it. And the whole time I was lying there flat, trying not to move a muscle, and everything on my body was itching. I just didn't feel like having a conversation with Brian today."

"Are you all right?" Laura asked.

Irene took a long breath and blew it out through puckered lips. "No, I'm not all right. And I'm not going to be all right for a while. But I'm not hurt either. You wouldn't think it would tire you out to lie in one spot and try not to move, but it does. Take my word for it. Did you see one of those bozos go around the lake?"

"Yeah, we saw him."

"That was the one that smashed his bike. Brian went to get the big guy. The other guy is supposed to make sure we don't try to take the path around the lake."

"It doesn't matter," Laura said. "We're not going that way anyway. You rest awhile. When you're ready to go, let me know."

"I'm never going to be ready. You kids go ahead and start anytime you want. I'll just poke along and do the best I can. Don't wait for me."

"We'll stay together," Laura said.

"That's stupid. You'd be a whole lot better off letting me come at my own pace."

"You'll do fine."

"I'm just going to hold everybody back," Irene said.

Laura moved away from her. "All right, let's get moving. We'll take it nice and easy. If you find a loose rock, pass the word behind you. Chris, will you go ahead? If we work toward the center of the slide, I think it'll be easier."

"Right," Chris said. He walked to his pack and raised it to his knee.

Laura moved next to Beverly and spoke to her quietly. "I'd like to have you carry your pack now. Irene needs a break."

Beverly turned toward her and stared. "You expect me to . . ." She raised her hand to the bandage on her forehead. "I don't think I can do it. My head really hurts."

"I know it does," Laura said. "But I want you to try to carry the pack for a while. We need your help."

Beverly turned away. "It's not fair. You just want to get back at me."

"Come on, Bev," Amy coaxed. "You can do it."

"Let's move out," Chris called to nobody in particular.

"I don't feel good at all," Beverly said. "It's not fair to make me carry a pack right now."

"Oh, cut it out," Amy snapped. "None of it's fair. It's not fair that we have to be climbing this dumb

rock pile in the first place. But you had to get started
with those creeps."

"It wasn't my fault," Beverly said. Somebody snorted.
"Well, it wasn't. I didn't know."

Chris came toward her. "Let's go, Bev. I'll help you
get your pack on."

"Well, I didn't know. I don't care what you people
think. It wasn't my fault. If Irene hadn't called him
names and pulled a knife . . ."

"Shut up, Bev," John said in a flat, emotionless
voice.

Chris held out Beverly's pack. "Stand up, and I'll
get the straps adjusted for you."

"I don't care what any of you think," Beverly said,
pulling herself to her feet. "It wasn't my fault, and
now I have a concussion, and not one of you cares."

"Shut up, Bev," John said again in the same bored
voice.

Chris slipped the pack onto Beverly's shoulders and
tightened the straps. "That feel all right?"

"What difference does it make?" Beverly muttered.

"Don't start that stuff with me," Chris said. "I want
to know if the straps are all right."

"I don't know, and I don't care."

"If you don't, I don't either." Chris turned toward
the others. "Let's get started."

Laura helped Irene to her feet. "Just do the best you
can, Irene."

"I will, honey. But I'm afraid that ain't any too good.

It just makes better sense for the rest of you to go on ahead."

"I don't feel good," Beverly said.

"Come on, Bev," Amy said. "Quit griping."

"Listen here," Irene shouted, "all of you lay off Beverly. She's hurting plenty. If she wants to gripe, let her. She's got it coming." She gave Beverly's arms a squeeze. "You try it with the pack for a while, sweetheart. Then I'll see if I can spell you."

The climb was slow and exhausting. They stepped from one rock to another, pulled themselves up over larger boulders, and retraced their steps when the way was too steep.

When Laura finally looked back, the lake was far below, and she had difficulty locating the spot where they had waited for Irene. But the top of the slide seemed as far away as ever.

They had moved onto a field of smaller boulders when Beverly slipped to her knees and then pitched forward and lay facedown on the rocks. "Are you all right, Bev?" Laura shouted as she dashed toward her. "Are you all right?" Beverly lay motionless.

Laura slipped off her pack and knelt beside Beverly. "Go away," Beverly moaned.

"It's okay, Bev," Laura said quietly. "We'll rest for a minute."

"Just go away. Leave me alone."

"What's the matter back there?" Amy called.

"We're taking a breather," Laura said.

"I want to die," Beverly moaned. "I just want to die."

"You'll feel better in a little while," Laura said. "It's a rough climb."

"I want to die," Beverly said again. "It's just not worth it. None of it is worth it. I just want to die."

The others, no longer wearing their packs, were making their way back. "Things will get better," Laura said.

Beverly continued to lie face down on the ground. "I don't care anymore. I just don't care."

"Is she hurt?" Stephanie asked Laura.

"She's exhausted."

"Why don't all of you go away and leave me alone?" Beverly said.

"Sit down and rest for a few minutes," Laura told the others. "It's time for a break anyway."

"I don't care how long we rest," Beverly said. "I'm not going any farther. It's not worth it."

"You'll change your mind," Laura said quietly.

Beverly began to moan. She wriggled her arms out of the pack and moved into a sitting position. "It just doesn't matter. Nothing matters at all. Don't you see? I just want to die." She was facing them, but her eyes did not seem to see them.

"Come on, Bev," Amy said disgustedly.

"Don't you see? I just want to die. Just leave me alone. I hate all of you, just the way you hate me. I don't care what you say. I just want to die." Her words began to catch in her throat until there were no more words, only moans.

The whole group sat and looked at Beverly and then at each other. Beverly sat, eyes glazed, moaning. Laura moved forward and put a hand on Beverly's shoulder. The others sat and fidgeted.

Irene stepped past Laura and sat down beside Beverly. "You're right, sweetheart," she said quietly. "Things are just so awful right now." And she began to cry. "Here you are, so tired and so hurt. It just breaks my heart because I can't do a thing about it." She put her arm around Beverly's waist. "I feel the same way you do, sweetheart. I want to die, too. I want them to go off and leave us alone. I just don't care either."

Laura sat back and watched the two of them, huddling together and crying. She felt her own throat tighten.

"Things are just so . . ." Beverly sobbed.

"I know it, kiddo," Irene wailed. "I know it."

Laura got up slowly and walked to Beverly's pack. She opened the main pouch and removed a plastic sack full of food packets. She took the sack to her own pack and stuffed it inside.

"Let me get some of that," Chris said. He reached into the pack and brought out the rolled-up tent. "I can tie this on the side of mine."

"Save some for me," John said, grabbing a sack of oatmeal.

"Out of the way," Donna said. "I saw that first."

"Stop it," Beverly said, reaching toward the pack. "I don't want you to take that stuff. It's . . . Oh, I don't know." She shook her head.

"Don't stop 'em now," Irene said through her tears. "They're doing fine. I figure if we cry long enough, they'll end up carrying us piggyback."

Beverly, still sobbing, looked at Irene and began to grin. Suddenly the two of them were laughing, with the tears still running down their cheeks. Laura and the others sat around awkwardly, almost as uncomfortable with the laughter as they had been with the crying.

"You're a mess," Irene said to Beverly.

"So are you," Beverly said, and laughed again.

"Aw, honey, I was never anything else. Not for a long time anyway."

Chris stood up and unfastened his canteen. "Anybody want a drink of water?"

When they started again, Beverly would not let Irene take her pack, even though Irene threatened to fight her for it. Chris led the way, moving at the same slow pace. Laura, taking her place at the end of the line, looked up and sighed. Things were better now, but there was still a long way to go.

Ten minutes later, when Chris called for a rest at a reasonably flat spot, they heard shouting from below. Laura looked toward the lake but could see no one.

"He's over where we started," Amy said. "Just on that first bunch of rocks. Look at the bottom of that far cliff, and then let your eyes move toward the lake from there."

Laura followed Amy's hand and finally located Brian. Once she could see him, it seemed easier to hear his words. "Come on down," he was shouting. "You can't get away."

"I'd tell him to go jump in the lake," Louie said, "but he might do it. And then I'd die of envy."

"We've come a long way," Chris said. "Look how far down he is."

"You can't get away," Brian yelled again.

"What's he talking about?" Donna asked.

"He says we can't get away," John muttered.

"I can hear him. I just want to know what he means."

Chris looked over at Laura. "He probably doesn't know about this way out. This isn't on any map, is it?"

"No," Laura said. "This is just something I heard about."

"Come on down," Brian was shouting.

"He's talking about something," Donna said, standing up. "He's got to be talking about something."

"Forget him," Chris said. "He's just making noise."

"Look," Donna shouted. "Look over there."

"What is it?" Chris asked. "What's the matter?"

"Just take a look," Donna said.

Far off to their left and a short distance below their level, a figure was climbing over the rocks, heading straight up the slide.

"It's Wally," Amy screamed. "It's Wally again."

"You can't get away," Brian shouted. "Come on down."

IX

Chris began to unbuckle his pack. "Some of us better try to cut up above him. If we can just get high ground on him, we can chase him back."

As Laura turned and watched Wally scramble over a boulder, she thought of Beverly with blood streaming down her forehead. "It's too late," she shouted.

Chris slipped out of his pack. "We gotta try it anyway."

"No!" Laura rushed forward and spoke directly to Chris. "If we have to fight, we'll do it. But not out here on the rockslide. This is the wrong place for a battle. And the last thing we need to do is to get split up, and that's what'll happen."

"We can't outclimb him," Chris said. "Not the whole bunch of us. So he'll end up cutting us off."

"You're right," Laura said. "So we won't go that way. Climbing the slide is out now."

"But what's left?"

"There's only one thing left," Laura said. "We'll cross the slide and get into that cave I told you about."

"A cave? But then we'll be trapped."

"Maybe. But wait'll you see it. The place is like a fort. There's no way they can get at us." She reached forward and picked up Chris's pack. "Please, Chris. Help us. We can't make it without you."

Chris rolled his eyes, but he grabbed the pack from her and pushed his arm through one strap. "All right. Whatever we're going to do, we'd better do it. How do we get there?"

"For a while we'll go straight across the slide, like we're trying to get away from Wally but still move up. Only we'll go straight across. We can probably drop a little without anybody noticing. When we get near the far side of the slide, we'll head straight down. The cave is just a little ways beyond the slide."

"You've been there?" Chris asked.

"Yes," Laura said, relieved that she could answer the question without lying. She *had* been to the cave. She hadn't been inside it because she had been afraid to make the trip along the narrow trail that led to the mouth. But things were different now.

They moved directly across the slide, no longer stopping to rest. Every few minutes Chris would look back at Laura, expecting the signal to move downhill. Finally he turned downhill without looking back. "We need to go down on an angle," he called over his shoulder.

"Keep your eye on that far cliff," Laura answered.

"We want to come off the slide right at the base of that cliff. There's a trail near there."

Moving downhill proved more difficult than Laura had thought. It was much easier to scramble up a large boulder than to try to slide down it on your stomach, your feet digging for some kind of hold. Laura found herself watching both above and below her. She expected Brian to appear at any time. Surely by this time he would have realized that something was happening. More frightening, however, was the possibility that Wally might be closing in upon them. After several painful slips Laura forced herself to watch the rocks in front of her. She settled on a hundred steps as a reasonable marker and then stopped—usually a few steps short—to check the surroundings. She could see nothing.

Suddenly the cliff loomed large in front of them. As they neared the edge of the slide, Laura was almost smiling while she picked her way over the smaller rocks.

"I thought there was a trail here," Chris said to her.

"There is. Maybe not right here, but soon enough. Just follow along the bottom of the cliff." She looked around. "All of you did great."

"Let's get moving," Chris said. "We're still out in the open."

"It's not far now," Laura said, wishing that her memory of the cave were a little clearer. She had not realized how close the base of the cliff was to the lakeshore. Myron had to be close by.

They had gone only about fifty yards when they stumbled onto the path leading up from the lake. They stood for a moment and stared down toward the water. "Wouldn't that be neat?" Louie said.

"Don't even think about it," Laura said. "No, that's dumb. Think about it all you want. Just don't do anything about it."

"Is it far now?" Chris asked her.

"No," Laura said, wishing things looked more familiar.

For a few minutes they followed the path—a rocky, eroded little trail between the nearly vertical cliffs above them and the sloping brushy hillside below. "I see it," Chris called. "Or I guess I do. There are a whole bunch of caves up there."

That section of the cliff was honeycombed with openings, most of them far too high to be accessible. Only one, Barker's Cave, was big enough and low enough to be named.

The hikers in front of her stopped, and Laura took one quick look behind her before she moved up to where Chris was standing, his head tilted back. "This must be the place," he said to her. "Wow."

The dark mouth of Barker's Cave was almost directly above them. From the base of the cliff, where they were standing, a narrow trail zigzagged upward for about thirty yards. Then, some twenty feet below the mouth of the cave, the trail seemed to stop, interrupted by an inaccessible overhang of rock.

Two years before, Laura had followed the trail up the cliff as far as that overhang. At that point she had decided to turn back. Looking at the terrain again, she fully understood that decision.

To get around the overhang, you had to veer far to the right, following a crack in the cliff. If you managed to claw your way far enough up the crack, you eventually reached the same horizontal layer of dark rock that made up the floor of the cave. This rock layer, more resistant to weather than the material above it, protruded about six inches out from the face of the mountain. If you were willing to tiptoe along this six-inch ledge, you could reach the cave.

"Do you see how the trail goes?" Laura asked. "You go up as far as that overhang, follow that crevice off to the right, and then come back along that ledge."

"That's what I was afraid of," Chris said.

"It's not as bad as it looks from here. We'll make it okay."

Chris didn't answer. He just stood and looked at the trail. The others began to gather around, their faces turned upward.

"No way," Louie said.

"Oh, Louie, come on," Amy said. "It's not that bad."

"Ladies first," Louie said.

"Suits me." Amy stepped past Chris and headed up

the path. "Who's coming with me?" Nobody answered her. "Oh, come on. We've got to get moving. You want to get caught out here in the open? John, come with me. You're not afraid, are you?"

"Of course not," Donna said. "His teeth always chatter that way."

"I'll come," John said, following Amy up the path.

Amy moved easily until she reached the overhang. She paused to study the crack in the rock for a moment and then climbed steadily to the top without stopping. She smiled down at the rest of them and then moved quickly along the ledge to the cave opening. Once there, she curtsied, lifting imaginary skirts as she dipped. "It's a piece of cake," she called down.

John took longer. Several times he stopped and seemed lost for a foothold. But he eventually found what he wanted and continued on. When he reached the ledge, he waited a long time, then inched his way across it. Every step seemed to be agony, but he kept moving until he was beside Amy.

"All right," Amy called. "The rest of you come on. The quarters aren't too spacious, but we have a nice view."

"Who's next?" Laura asked.

"You're elected," Chris said.

"Who's coming with me? Louie? Donna? Stephanie?"

"Oh, I'll come," Donna said. "If klutzo can make it, I can, too."

"Let's all go," Laura said. "There's no use waiting around. You have to do it sooner or later." She turned and started up the trail, hoping that some of the others would come with her.

Laura did not like high places. She didn't know whether she was more afraid of falling than anyone else or whether it was natural to get a queasy stomach when you looked down from the top of a building or a bridge. Now, however, there was no choice. She had to make the climb, and she had to keep from showing her fear.

Someone had once told Laura that the secret of climbing was never to look down. Having no experience of her own to draw upon, she resolved to follow that rule religiously.

The first part of the path was steep and rough, but no worse than climbing the rockslide. When she stopped at the overhang to catch her breath, she was feeling a surge of confidence. "Come on," she called down to the others. "Let's get going." Only Donna had started up the path. The rest stood in a half circle, looking upward.

Once Laura began to move along the break in the rock, her confidence dissipated. There was nothing substantial to get a grip on. Her feet kept slipping on the slick cliff, and the sharp edges of the crack seemed to be ripping the flesh from her hands.

But she continued to move upward, driven along by the knowledge that there was nothing else to do. When her foot slipped, she held onto the rock face with a strength that she didn't know she possessed. She couldn't let go, no matter how badly her fingers ached. She pulled herself higher, promising her hands relief when she reached the top.

And then she was on the ledge. She leaned against the cliff, opening and closing her hands. Her muscles were still cramping, but it was an enormous relief not to have to hold onto anything.

Hearing Donna puffing, Laura turned and looked down at her. Donna was struggling along, her teeth clenched. Laura looked below at the empty path and then at the hikers still huddled in a half circle at the base of the cliff. She felt her stomach contract and her knees soften. She gripped the rocks beside her with both hands. Her feet were secure, but she was still in danger because she could not control her muscles.

"Steady," she whispered. "Keep it steady." After a minute she felt herself relaxing once more. She kept her eyes focused on the rock cliff that she was facing.

"Can you move, Laura?" Donna said from below. "I'm not sure I can make it up while you're standing there."

It took Laura a moment to answer. There was nothing ahead of her but an absurdly narrow ledge. The cliff was too sheer for handholds. She would have to move across that ledge with only her feet to keep her in place. "I'm on my way," she said softly.

"That's good." Donna sighed. "I need all the room I can get right now."

Facing the cliff, Laura began to work her way along the ledge. Her pack seemed enormously heavy, heavy enough to pull her over backward. She kept her hands and forearms on the rock face, even though there was nothing to grasp. Her balance seemed more secure with her hands high.

She had an enormous fear of removing a foot from the ledge. It seemed that if she lifted one foot, even for an instant, she would lose her equilibrium. So she slid her left foot an inch or two and then matched that with the right. Then the left; then the right. She seemed not to be moving at all, even though she was dimly aware that Donna was now perched on the ledge.

"Keep coming, Laura," Amy called. "You're doing great."

Laura pressed her cheek against the rock face for a minute before sliding her left foot sideways once more. All time seemed to have stopped. Her body, originally tense, now seemed numb and out of control. Her right foot scraped along until it touched the left. Then the left foot began to move again.

"A little more, Laura. Just a little more." Amy's voice was encouraging but maddening in its casual tone. Didn't Amy realize, Laura wondered, just how dangerous this was? "A few steps more. Keep it moving."

Then John's hand was holding her forearm, and Laura took the final steps to where the ledge suddenly joined the cave floor. "Thank you," she said mechanically, and turned away. She desperately wanted to lie down, but she wanted to do so where the people below couldn't see her.

"Watch your head," John told her. "You can't stand up inside."

Laura turned and smacked her head against the roof of the cave. "I see what you mean," she said, and managed a smile. She bent over and moved away from the ledge.

"Make yourself at home," Amy said.

Laura was amazed to see how small the cave actually was. Ten feet wide and five feet high at the mouth, it had seemed enormous from below. Now she could see how that huge mouth had misled her.

The cave looked like a wedge hacked out of the mountain by a gargantuan ax. The farther from the mouth you moved on the flat floor, the lower you had to stoop. It was probably forty feet from the mouth to the place where the slanting roof finally met the floor, but you would have to crawl on your stomach for the final ten feet.

Donna ducked into the cave and sank down on the floor beside Laura. "I don't know about you," she said, "but I'm glad to be here."

"Come on, you guys," Amy was shouting. "You can make it. Chris, what about you?"

"Don't worry about me," he called back. "But I'll come up last, just in case."

"Too bad we don't have a rope," Amy muttered.

"You know," John said, "I'll bet we could get together enough string and cord out of our boots and our tents and sleeping bags so that we could at least pull up the packs. I don't know about you, but it would have been a lot easier for me if I hadn't had to carry anything."

Donna moaned. "Now you think of it. There I was, dying out there, thinking about my dainty little body being splattered across the rocks. And now that I'm here, you start having brainstorms."

With a little prodding the rest of the group came up the trail as far as the overhang. Laura was relieved to have them there. Even if Brian appeared now—and she kept expecting him—he would be directly below them and powerless to attack.

Once the cord was ready, John tied one end to a small rock and tossed the rock over the edge. In a matter of minutes all of the packs were lined up against the far side of the cave. "How about that for knot tying?" John said. "Not a single break."

"You're fantastic," Donna said. "I told them they shouldn't have kicked you out of Campfire Girls."

Laura knelt at the front of the cave and tried to peer over the edge. "You can't get far enough out to see," Amy said. "I already tried. You don't need to look, though. I can tell you what they're doing—

standing there." She knelt beside Laura and shouted, "Get moving down there. There's nothing to it. Louie, Stephanie, go ahead."

"I don't know if I can make it," Louie said. "I'm not sure I can fit." Laura was surprised at how close he sounded.

"Nothing to it, Louie," Amy said. "You could do it blindfolded." She turned to Laura and whispered, "It doesn't sound too hopeful, does it?"

"Keep after them," Laura said. "They'll come."

"I think I'll go down and hustle them along," Amy said. "Don't go away."

"Don't worry," Laura said.

Amy moved to the ledge, faced the cliff, and started off. Laura stood and watched, totally amazed at the performance. Amy was across the ledge in little more time than it would have taken her to walk that distance on a sidewalk. Then she slid down the crack in the rock and disappeared from Laura's view.

"I hate a showoff," John said, "but she's fantastic."

"All right," Amy was saying. "Let's head up there. Louie, you go first. Then Irene. Then Bev."

"I can't do it," Beverly shouted. "I just can't do it. I'll fall. I know I'll fall."

"No, you won't," Amy said. "But you can stay here for a minute. Once Irene and Louie are up, I'll come back for you." Louie was still standing in the same spot. "Louie, do you want me ahead of you or behind you?"

"What's the third choice?"

"No third choice. Do you want me to go ahead and show you where to put your hands?"

"Yeah," Louie said.

"Irene?"

"It doesn't matter, honey. I might as well tag along behind. Then when I fall, I won't land on anybody."

"Nobody's going to fall," Amy said. "Let's go."

For a while Laura watched the slow progress up the crack. Finally she could not bear to look any longer. Louie was going to make it, but it was just too hard for Laura to stand by helplessly and watch the painfully deliberate moves.

She sat back and gazed out at the lake, trying to ignore the sounds below her. As her eyes moved beyond the still water, she spotted a flash of color and then another. Listening carefully, she could hear the faint hum of engines.

When Louie finally reached the ledge, Laura moved back into the cave and rummaged in her pack so that she wouldn't have to watch. She was still there when Amy shouted, "Good going, Louie. I knew you could make it." Louie stepped onto the cave floor and dropped to his knees. A moment later Irene stepped over him and moved beside Laura.

"How are you doing?" Laura asked her.

"I don't know, honey. I'm all right, I guess. I just gave myself up for dead out there, and after that it was easier. I just decided I was going to die and there was no use worrying about it. Now that I'm up here, I have to get used to the idea of being alive again."

"Laura," Amy said, "I think we've got a basket case on our hands. Bev is scared to death down there."

"I don't blame her," Irene said.

"She may settle down," Laura told Amy.

"Sit down and cry with her," Irene muttered. "It helped once."

"Hey, John," Amy said, "do you think there's any way to tie together two sleeping bags?"

"I don't know. There might be."

"See what you can do."

While John worked on the sleeping bags, Laura kept watching the motorcycles circle the lake. She decided to say nothing for the moment. There was nothing to be gained from telling the others.

"Chris and Stephanie," Amy called down, "you two come ahead. You might as well come now and get out of the way. Hang on, Bev. We're going to take care of you."

"It doesn't work, Amy," John said. "Even if I use cord, they're too bulky and too slick. I'd hate to bet they'd stay together."

"That's okay," Amy said. She leaned out over the edge. "Way to go, Chris. Just keep moving now." She bent over and walked back to where Laura was sitting. "Laura, you're elected."

"For what?"

"I need somebody to help me with Bev, and you're the best climber."

"It was all an act," Laura said. "I was scared to death."

"*Everybody* is," Amy said, "but some get bothered more than others. You ought to see Chris out there. He's having a tough time. Stephanie's all right, but Chris is suffering. And it's worse for him because he's still trying to be the tough guy."

"How are you going to manage Bev?" Laura asked.

"I'm not too sure. I was trying to figure out a way to pull her up or to keep her from falling. But it just can't be done. She's got to do it herself. But if we make her think she's safe, it should be better."

"And I have to go down and come up again?"

"I think I can get her as far as the ledge," Amy said. "It's just on the ledge that I'll need help."

"I have trouble out there," Laura said.

"Sure you do. So do I. But you can handle yourself."

Laura could think of nothing to say.

Once Chris and Stephanie were in the cave, Amy wrapped a sleeping bag around her shoulders and started back across the ledge. When she reached the crack, she left the sleeping bag and slid down the rock. Laura moved slowly across the ledge, reminding herhelf never to look down. Near the middle she remembered Brian and started to glance toward the lake, but she caught herself before she did.

As she inched along, using the same sideways motion she'd used before, she could hear Amy below her, sometimes coaxing, sometimes badgering. If Beverly was saying anything at all, Laura couldn't hear her.

Laura found herself thinking of Irene's comment about deciding that she was going to die. That wasn't the way that Laura would put it, but she knew what Irene meant. You had to accept what you were doing, danger and all. You were still frightened, and your stomach still hurt, but you stayed in control.

Laura was concentrating so hard on each step that she did not realize that she was across until her leg brushed against the sleeping bag. She knelt down and moved the bag aside. There where the crack met the ledge, one person could stand comfortably. Two could probably squeeze into the space. Laura didn't know what they would do when there were three of them. Leaning against the rock and making herself concentrate on her balance, she looked down at Beverly and Amy. Beverly's face was white, her eyes glazed. Amy was just below her, chattering instructions and encouragement.

"Get your weight on your left foot now. Get all of your weight on it. I'm going to move your right foot up about six inches. There's a good toehold there. Can you find it on your own? No? Okay. Don't worry about it. Just get your weight on your left foot. Let the right one relax, and I'll move it for you. Here we go. That's it."

And so it went. Laura stood and waited, helpless for the moment. When Beverly drew close, Laura braced herself and held out a hand. Beverly looked at her and did not move. "It's okay, Bev," she said. "You have it made now." She reached down and took Beverly's wrist and gently pulled. For a moment Beverly seemed to sag, and Laura was afraid that Beverly was going to let go of everything. "Keep your feet working, Bev. I can give you a hand, but I can't hold you." Beverly's arm seemed limp, and Laura thought of the packs they had pulled up earlier. At that point Beverly was little different, just heavier.

"Come on, Bev," Amy said. "You've got it made now. Lift your left foot a long ways up. There's a place there for you to dig in. Lift it up now. I can't reach it, but you can do it. Lift it up. Higher. Higher."

Laura could feel Beverly strain and then relax as she changed position. "All right, Bev. If you grab hold right here, you can pull yourself up." Beverly seized the handhold, pulled herself forward, and then grabbed Laura.

"Laura," she said, squeezing her tightly. "I was so . . ."

"You made it," Laura said. "You did great." She hugged Beverly uneasily, trying to steady both of them.

"Now comes the easy part," Amy said from below. "We just have to go over to the cave now. No more hard climbing."

Beverly looked at the ledge and began to sob. "I can't.

I can't go any farther. I'm dizzy. I'm sorry, Amy, but I think I'm going to faint."

"Everybody gets like that once in a while," Amy said. "You've done great. I thought you were going to be a problem, but you're one heck of a climber. This is the easy part now. You had to do the first part on your own, but now we can help. Laura, you'll need to get the sleeping bag and move out onto the ledge so that I can get up there. See, Bev, we're going to be on each side of you, and we're going to hold you on the ledge with the sleeping bag. You won't have a thing to worry about."

"I—I—I," Beverly mumbled. Laura waited, but nothing followed.

"Go ahead, Laura," Amy said. "No use waiting around."

Laura took one end of the sleeping bag and made her way out onto the ledge. Almost immediately Amy was up beside Beverly. "See how it works best for you, Laura," Amy said. "You may want to hold the bag in your right hand, or you may want to bring it around your back and hold it there with your left arm." Laura passed the bag across her back and held it in place with her arm. There was nothing to hang onto, but she felt more secure with her right arm free.

It was awkward at first, and each small tug caused Laura to tense all of her muscles. Once they were started, however, the movement was easier. Strangely enough, Laura found a certain reassurance in the bag across her back and in the body pressed close to her. It was more awkward, of course, but less frightening somehow.

Laura took the same deliberate sidesteps as before, and the others seemed to be following. She did not look at them. She stared at the cliff in front of her.

When the first shouts came, Laura ignored them. She was completely absorbed in her trek across the ledge. Only when Beverly stopped moving did the shouts from below start to register. "Hey, Beverly. What's going on up there?"

Laura felt Beverly twist away from her, and the sleeping bag yanked. "Keep going," Amy shouted. "You're doing fine. Don't stop now."

"I—I—I," Beverly began.

"Move it," Amy said.

"I—I—I."

"Don't look down," Laura said. "Bev, settle down."

"I—I can't. . . ."

"Look, you moronic goose," Amy screamed, "we can't hold you on here. If you start to go, we'll let go of the bag. So if you want to be around tomorrow, quit wiggling and start moving. Otherwise, make it easy on us. Just tell us first and then jump. You want to do that?"

"No," Beverly moaned.

"All right then. Move. Ignore that idiot down there. Just take it a step at a time. You can do it. You've been doing great up till now."

"Come on, Bev," Laura said. "I'm going to take a step now, and I want you to do the same. Here we go. Step. Then the other foot. Step. Now the first one. Step." Laura could feel Beverly moving along, but she could also feel Beverly's involuntary shaking, a jerking which threatened to topple all of them.

"You guys are so dumb," Brian yelled. "What're you trying to prove anyway?"

"Step," Laura shouted. "Now the other foot. Step. Now the first one."

"That's the way," Amy said. "You're doing great."

"I—I—I," Beverly began.

"Don't try to talk," Laura said. "Just keep moving with me. We're almost there. Ready now. Step. Other foot. Step."

Laura continued to stare at the rock directly in front of her. She knew that they must be getting close to the cave, but she did not dare turn. As she called out the cadence, her voice grew louder and louder. Part of her shouting was for Beverly. At least it had started that way. After a while it was for Laura herself. It gave her a way to release the fear and anxiety that were bottled up inside her. "Step. Now the first foot. Step. Now the other. Step."

Behind her Amy was chattering, and below her Brian would yell occasionally, but Laura paid no attention. Her whole world was reduced to her own shouts and her timed movements. "Now the first foot. Step. Now the other. Step."

When Laura felt someone grasp her arm, she had to fight to keep herself upright. Her whole body wanted to collapse. "All right, Bev. We're here. I'm going to take your arm now and help you in."

"Don't touch me!" Beverly screamed. "You'll make me fall!"

"All right," Laura said. "First foot. Step. Now the other. Step. Now the first again. Step." By this time Laura was standing on the cave floor. She reached out, quickly grasped Beverly's arm, and pulled her forward.

Amy scooted past them. "Nice going, Bev. You did great."

Beverly stood with her arms at her sides and stared straight ahead of her. She started to speak, but when she opened her mouth, she could only sob. "Help her back here," Irene said. "She just needs to rest for a while."

"Watch your head, Bev," Donna said, leading her back into the cave.

"Right here, kiddo," Irene said. "Bring that sleeping bag, somebody. Now you lie down here for a few minutes. You'll feel better in a little while. You've had some kind of a terrible day." Irene began to smooth Beverly's hair as she wrapped the sleeping bag around her.

"Hey, Laura," Brian yelled from below. "Whatcha gonna do now? Sooner or later you gotta come down."

"Everybody come back away from the entrance,"

Laura said. "As long as he has an audience, he'll go on indefinitely."

"Did little Beverly hurt her head today?" he yelled. "She better come down here so I can give her some first aid." He laughed loudly, an artificial shrieking. "Then she can give *me* some first aid."

"I mean it," Laura said. "Chris, John, come on back. I don't want him to be able to see anybody."

"Wally wants to come up and visit," Brian yelled. "He's got a thing for that little half-pint." Again he shrieked.

"Let's toss down a rock or two," Chris said, "just to give him something to think about."

"No, Chris," Laura said. "He's just making noise. That's all he can do."

"But we don't need it," Chris said, turning away from her.

"It's just noise. The less attention we pay to him, the sooner he'll get bored and go away."

"How much food and water you got, Laura?" Brian yelled. "How long can you hold out up there? You get hungry, you just send the half-pint down. Wally'll share his dinner with her."

Laura looked around her. Irene and Beverly were sitting on the floor of the cave, staring at the entrance. Chris was on his knees beside Stephanie, who seemed to be crying. Amy was far back in the cave, crouched down low. Laura shook her head, wondering if they would feel better if they all rolled rocks down the hill.

"We're gonna wait for you guys," Brian shouted. "I don't care how long it is. We'll still be here. When you get thirsty enough and hungry enough, you'll come down. And we'll be here."

Laura knew that she had to do something. "Everybody gather around," she said, moving beside Beverly. "Right now. Come over here and sit in a circle. Come on." They came reluctantly. "Gather around. I want everybody to hold hands." She reached out and took Beverly's hand on one side and John's on the other. "Now just keep holding hands for a minute." She spoke loudly, drowning out the shouts from below. "I'm thankful that we're all here and that we're all safe. I'm thankful for the courage that each of you showed. I'm proud of every one of you, and you have a right to be proud of yourselves." Hearing no more shouts, she concluded, "And don't worry. We're going to get out of here all right."

"How?" Chris asked after a moment of silence.

"First things first. Right now we all need a good meal. It's been a long time since breakfast. Then we're going to sleep. I can't imagine that even Brian and Wally are stupid enough to try to come up that trail, but we'll keep two people on watch. The rest of us will sleep. Once we're fed and rested, we'll worry about the next step."

"I don't see . . ." Chris began.

"Not now, Chris. Right now we're all exhausted. You people have done more work today than any human beings should have to do. And it's not even noon yet. We're going to eat, and then we're going to sleep. I don't want any questions or worrying or negative thoughts. We're tired and hungry. Let's take care of those problems first."

Once the meal was cooking, Amy pulled Laura off to the side. "Laura," she whispered, "we've got a problem."

"I said no worrying until after we ate and slept."

"This may not wait," Amy said. "We don't have any bathroom here."

Laura almost laughed but stopped herself when she saw Amy's face. "You're right." She studied the cave, although she knew it was hopeless. There were no outcroppings, no convenient boulders.

"You see what I mean?" Amy said.

"Everybody gather around," Laura said. "This will just take a minute."

"Don't turn down the fire," Louie said. "Keep that food going."

"Listen," Laura said as the group gathered, "we're not exactly staying at the Sheraton here. We don't have a bathroom, and we don't have any way to make one. So when you need a bathroom, get two others to go with you, and they can each hold up one end of this blanket here. And we can do without the comments and wisecracks. It's the best we can do, and we'll have to put up with it. We'll use that far back corner of the cave as our spot. It's not classy, but it's the best we can do."

"Give me that blanket," Irene said. "The old lady gets first chance. Donna, Stephanie—give me a hand."

The boys drifted to the front of the cave and stood staring out toward the lake. "End of problem," Laura told Amy.

"It's still kind of creepy, just being behind a blanket that way."

"Sure it is," Laura said, "but we'll manage."

"You know what those yo-yos are doing now?" Louie called over his shoulder. "They're swimming."

"All three of them?" Laura asked.

"I can only see two," Louie said. "I don't know where the third guy is."

"I'll bet he's watching the cave," Amy said, tears welling up in her eyes.

X

"Time for some food," Laura called. "Come on, all you sack rats. It's time you were up and cooking."

It was only six thirty, but already the light in the cave was growing dim. Laura had taken over guard duty at four, along with Louie. She had slept solidly until then and was in no danger of sleeping again, so she had told Louie to go back to sleep.

Most of the crew had crawled into their sleeping bags as soon as lunch was over and had not stirred since. Even when Brian and Wally had come to the bottom of the trail to yell, almost nobody heard. Laura was not sure whether the cave shut out some of the sound from below or whether exhaustion was the major factor. At any rate she might have been the only one who heard them. She hoped so. The yells were playful at first, then gradually more obscene when nobody responded.

Laura had stayed out of sight while the two of them were yelling. As she had hoped, they soon tired without an audience and left.

"Up and at 'em," she called.

Louie sat up in his sleeping bag. "You're the ideal partner for watch duty," he said. "We make a great team."

"No problem," Laura said. "I had slept all I could by then."

"I managed to force myself to rest a little more," Louie said, and laughed. "It was a struggle, but I made it."

"Come on," Laura said. "I'm getting hungry."

"What time is it?" somebody called. "It's almost dark."

Irene crawled out of her sleeping bag and walked barefoot to the front of the cave where Laura was sitting. "You mean I slept the whole afternoon?"

"I don't think you moved."

"Well, I feel a little better now. Just wish I could stand up straight and stretch. What do you feel like eating?"

"Let's have the best of whatever we have. And lots of it."

Irene moved closer to Laura. "You think we ought to take it a little easy on the food, in case we end up having to be here awhile?"

"I don't think those guys will last much longer," Laura said.

The boys were back in the corner of the cave, holding the blanket for each other. "Amy," Louie yelled, "quit trying to peek."

"You're disgusting," Amy said, moving to the front of the cave beside Laura. "Nobody called me for guard duty."

"You earned your sleep."

"I wish I was still asleep. I hate this place."

"You'll like it better," Irene said, "when you see what we got for supper."

When the meal was served, everyone sat at the mouth of the cave. It was too dark inside to see what was on the plates. The only sounds were the clanking of utensils on metal dishes.

Laura was thinking about water as she ate. There was no shortage of drinking water yet, but there was no extra water for dishwashing. By the next day water would be scarce.

"I've been thinking," John said suddenly.

"That's a change," Donna said.

"Why couldn't we tie together tents? Sleeping bags are too bulky and slick, but there ought to be a way to lash together the tents—the good ones anyway."

"Give it a try," Laura said. "Somebody get a flashlight and hold it for John."

"I don't need a light yet," John said, "but I probably will pretty soon."

"How do we wash our plates?" Stephanie asked.

"Get the paper towels," Irene said. "Use the towels to wipe off the plates, and then scrape all the extra junk into a plastic bag. Not too sanitary, but it'll do."

Two groups quickly formed—one working with the

tents, the other scraping the dishes. Irene and Laura sat and watched. "I guess age has its privileges," Irene said.

"Hey," came a shout from below, "how's it going up there?"

"Just ignore him," Laura said. "He'll go away sooner that way."

"Hey, half-pint," Brian shouted, "come on down. Wally's lonesome for somebody to play with."

"Keep an eye on the path," Chris said to Laura. "Be sure they aren't trying to sneak up close enough to throw rocks."

Laura looked over the edge. Brian was standing far below, where the brush met the rocky cliff.

"It's gotta be boring up there in that cave," he shouted. "You better come on down. We'll have some fun. Beverly, how's your pretty little head? Come on down, and I'll kiss it and make it better." He laughed loudly. "Good thing it hit you in the head. Can't do any damage there."

Laura could sense the uneasiness in the cave. Dishes were still being scraped, and somebody was stretching out a tent, but all attention seemed to be focused on the shouts.

"Hey, Laura, ask that wimpy dude how his stomach feels today. No wonder he's up there hiding in a cave. One punch, and I had him on the ground crying for his mommy."

Laura looked quickly back at Chris, who was kneeling beside a folded tent. Then she caught herself. It was silly for her to allow this to happen. She began to sing loudly, "You got to walk that lonesome valley. You got to walk it by yourself." The others joined in heartily, and the cave echoed with the music. Brian shouted louder, but Laura couldn't make out his words.

They continued to sing verse after verse, changing the name each time. Laura kept watching Brian. For a while he shouted. Then he stood stiffly and waited. When the song continued on and on, he picked up a pair of rocks and began to scramble up the path toward the overhang.

Laura snatched a rock from the pile they had gathered and leaned forward, her arm cocked. She felt her body grow rigid as all of her stored-up anger seemed to surface at once. Yet, as her hand came forward, she wavered and purposely sent the rock too far to the left. She reached toward the pile again.

As Laura's rock bounced past him, Brian stopped, threw his own rocks, and ran back downhill. The rocks which he threw struck the cliff below the mouth of the cave and came bouncing back down toward him. He shouted something and shook his fist before he turned and left.

"Okay," John called, "stop singing long enough to try this out. I want half of you on one side and half on the other. I want you to hold on and pull. Actually, don't worry about pulling. What I want you to do is get your weight behind it. So get a good hold and lean back."

It was a strange sort of tug-of-war game. No one could stand up straight, and the floor was too slick for a decent foothold. Whenever one side began to move the other, John would shout orders for a change in teams. After they had pulled at three or four different spots, John took a flashlight and studied his work.

"If we can't pull it apart that way," he said as he ran his hands over the knots, "then it ought to work all right. It's over two feet longer than the cord we used to pull up the packs, so it should be long enough."

"You're not as dumb as you look," Donna said.

"That's great, John," Laura said. "It's better than I could have hoped for."

"But how do we use it?" Chris wanted to know.

"Well, see," Louie said, "we hold it out, and that dingdong down there climbs up it. And then, when he gets almost to the top, we let go."

"Why don't I make some cocoa?" Irene said.

"Hey," Brian yelled from below, "is Beverly all right? Come on, up there. Don't start in singing. Just tell me—is Beverly all right?"

Beverly looked over at Laura. "Am I supposed to answer him?"

"I don't know, Bev," Laura said. "What do you think?"

Beverly looked around at the others, then moved to

the mouth of the cave. "Brian? I'm all right. I have this cut on my head." She raised her hand to her forehead. "It hurts, but it's not too bad."

"Hey, foxy," he shouted, "what do you think? You think I ought to forget about what those guys did to me? You think we ought to just pack up and leave you alone? Just head on out of here?"

"Yes," Beverly called. "Oh, yes. Please, Brian. Would you do that?"

"Hey, tell you what. You get all of your people there to come out and say they're sorry, and I'll go."

"Come on, Brian."

"I mean it. I figure they owe me that much. What's the matter? They too high and mighty up there to admit they can make a mistake?"

"Are you kidding?"

"Hey, listen, foxy, I'm serious. It's not gonna hurt any of 'em. You get them all to come out and say they're sorry, and we'll go."

Beverly looked back at the others. "It's worth a try," Laura said. "You don't have to mean it."

"Just a second," Beverly called. "We're coming."

"I want the old lady, too. She's the one I want to hear the loudest."

"I know what I'd like to tell him," Irene muttered, but she came forward with the others.

They formed a row at the front of the cave, some stooping and some on their knees. Once there, nobody seemed to know how to begin. Laura looked down to where Brian stood in the twilight. "Brian," she called, "we're sorry."

"Let's hear it from all of them," Brian shouted. "I want to hear it good and loud."

"All right," Laura said. "Let's do it on three. One. Two. Three."

Like a cheering section, they boomed out, "We're sorry."

"You people crack me up," Brian shouted. "Now you figure I'm gonna go away and leave you alone and forget about what you did, right? You said you were sorry, and now everything's fine, right? Well, forget it, you turkeys. I just wanted to make sure you were all there. And I wanted to see how dumb you were. And you came through for me like champs. You think you're gonna get off that easy, you're out of your mind. Hey, Beverly, you brainless—"

"Let's sing," Laura shouted, moving back into the cave. She began "Kumbayah," and the others joined in. By the time that they were through all of the verses the cocoa was ready and Brian was silent.

"If we hear anything more from him tonight," Chris said, "we ought to throw a few rocks in his direction. That'll make him think a little before he comes too close."

"I don't think you need to worry about him any more tonight," Laura said.

"But what about tomorrow?"

"We'll see," she said.

They sat in a circle around the stove and sipped their cocoa. Laura could sense all of them watching her. Now that they were rested, they were looking to her for guidance. She wished that she had more of a plan to offer them.

"Before daylight tomorrow," she said finally, "we're going to send somebody out of here. It will be rough going for the first couple of miles, but they'll need to get away from the lake before it gets light. After that it'll be a long walk, but there shouldn't be any problems. They should be able to get to the car by early afternoon. I don't know whether help can get here by tomorrow night, but it doesn't really matter. We can hold out here as long as we have to."

"But won't they have Wally up on the trail again?" Stephanie asked.

"Look," Laura said, "you know what this place is like. Do you think Brian's going to expect anybody to climb down from here in the dark?"

"Which brings up another question," Louie said. "How are we going to get somebody to climb down from here in the dark?"

Laura smiled and sipped her cocoa. "They get their choice, I think. Either they climb down John's rope, or we lower them down."

"Next question," Louie went on. "Who's going?"

"Are you volunteering, Louie?" Donna asked.

"I'll go," Chris said.

"Me, too," Stephanie announced.

"Hold on a minute," Chris said. "I'm not about to—"

"Hold it," Laura ordered. "We have some time to think. Let's work on it for a while."

None of them argued. In fact, none of them spoke at all. The whole group sat in silence for several minutes. Laura wished they had a fire, both for warmth and to pick up their spirits. As darkness settled over the lake, it brought a sense of gloom with it.

"All right," Laura said finally, "there's nothing we can do for a while, and it's cold. Everybody get some sleep. We'll keep two people on guard duty, mostly so that we don't all go to sleep and wake up about noon tomorrow."

There was surprisingly little resistance. Within fifteen minutes everybody was settled in a sleeping bag except Irene and Beverly. Laura had offered to replace either of them, but they both insisted on a turn at guard duty. "We're volunteering for this," Irene said to Laura, "but you won't hear us volunteering to hike out for help."

Laura lay in her sleeping bag and tried to think. She could hear Beverly and Irene whispering, and she could hear somebody's heavy breathing. She had decisions to make: How many people should she send for help? And which ones? She had to send somebody who could drive. John and Donna were sixteen and had drivers' licenses. She wasn't sure about any of the others. Should she go herself? Irene could keep things going in the cave. There were so many things to decide, and the sleeping bag was so warm.

Laura was awakened by a hand on her shoulder. She sat up quickly. "What time is it?" she whispered.

"Midnight," Irene answered. She moved away from Laura.

Laura pulled on her boots, wishing she had laces, and slipped into her jacket, which she had been using for a pillow. She made her way to the front of the cave, which seemed enormously bright. She stepped into the moonlight and looked down at the lake, shining silver in the distance.

"They're all quiet," Irene said. "They've been quiet for an hour or so now. Bright as the moon is, we figured maybe somebody ought to do something."

"We think all three of them are together," Beverly said, "but we can't be sure of it."

"We kept listening and listening," Irene explained. "We couldn't pick up the words, but after a while we got so we could catch voices. That one guy doesn't talk much, so it's hard to tell about him."

"I wish I knew what to do," Laura said.

"It's a tough one, honey. Beverly and I've been working on it all night, and we don't have any real good answers."

"We don't know if the path is blocked or not,"

Beverly said. "One of them might be down there. We just don't know for sure."

Laura looked down at the lake again. "I wish I knew."

"We've had some time to think about it," Irene said. "We were thinking it might be a good idea to send a bunch down to check out the path. Not just one person—send a little help along, in case the quiet guy's out there."

"That sounds like a good idea," Laura said.

"I don't really think there's going to be any trouble, but we probably need to check before we send somebody off. And then, while that bunch is down there, they can get more water. Otherwise, things might be a little tight tomorrow. When we're sure things are clear, we can figure out who to send—just so it's not me."

"Good," Laura said, glad to have someone else thinking clearly.

"I'll start waking people up," Irene said. She moved back into the cave. Laura could hear her moving from place to place. "Come on. Get up and get your shoes on. But be quiet about it."

In three minutes they had formed a semicircle in the moonlight. Laura was still uncertain, but Irene's idea was better than any she had. "What we'll do is send three people down to get water and check out the path—to make sure we can get out without any trouble."

"What we figured," Beverly broke in, "is that John, Amy, and somebody else ought to go. They're lighter, and they'll be easier for the rest of us to hold."

"Thanks a lot," John said. "I hope I can return the favor sometime."

"I'll go along with them," Laura said. "I'm heavier, but not that much. No comments, please. You can hold me. But I have to get some shoelaces first."

While she was tying her shoes, Chris brought the lashed-together tents and began to feed them over the side. "You'd rather climb down, wouldn't you, Laura? If we try to lower you down, you'll get bumped on all the rocks."

"Whatever you say, Chris. I'm brand-new at this business."

"I have all the water bottles in one pack," Irene said. "That's probably the easiest."

Once the bulky rope was played out, and the others stood, braced to take the weight, Laura shrugged and said, "I might as well go first. After me, the others won't seem so bad." She buckled on the pack and sat down at the front of the cave, letting her feet swing over the edge. She turned onto her stomach, took the tent rope in hand, and began to work her way down. "Hold steady," she whispered.

For some distance, movement was easy. She simply backed down the steep slope, using the rope to hold herself upright. But then there was only empty space when she reached for another step. She lay down flat and began to work her way over the edge. Her arms were aching, and she was afraid that she would not be able to hold her weight without help from her feet.

As she was easing herself over the edge, a long-forgotten picture flashed through her mind: She was seven or eight, and she and the neighbor boy would climb the stop sign on the corner and then slide down. Suddenly Laura began to smile. She wrapped her legs around the rope and then eased herself down. It was harder on her hands and slower, but she held onto that picture of the stop sign until she felt earth beneath her feet. She let go of the rope for a moment, then gave two sharp pulls to let them know that she was down. It had not been sheer pleasure, but it was certainly better than scooting along the ledge.

She stood and waited, listening for any noises from below. Now that she was safely down from the cave, the other dangers could be dealt with. Before that, nothing but the descent seemed to matter.

Hearing scraping and scuffling above her, Laura moved to the side and looked up to see a body coming toward her. "Look out below," John whispered as he slid to the ground. He gave two tugs on the rope and turned to Laura. "I came down a little faster than I meant to, but it wasn't too bad. We'd better move back. Knowing Amy, she'll probably jump."

There were the same scraping and sliding sounds as before, and a figure appeared above them, moving hand over hand down the rope. "Here I am," Amy said, as her feet touched the ground. "Anything happening down here?"

"No, thank goodness," Laura said. "Let's go. We'll try to get by without a flashlight if we can. We can see pretty well right now."

The moonlight proved to be surprisingly deceptive. Even at the start, when the trail down the cliff seemed bathed in light, Laura found herself stumbling and sliding until she quit trusting her eyes. Once she began feeling her way, making certain of each foothold, she moved more quietly and more easily.

The next section of the trail was in shadow, but there was little danger of losing the path because there was brush on one side and the cliff on the other. The three of them moved more quickly then, walking with their hands stretched out to the sides.

When the path moved away from the cliff and down toward the water, Laura resisted the temptation to use her flashlight. There just might be someone to see it. She made her way slowly down the steep incline, sometimes by sight, usually by feel.

Near the water's edge the downhill path merged with the fishermen's trail that circled the lake. Laura stopped at the junction and looked across the water to where a campfire still glowed. John came up beside her and whispered in her ear. "It looks all clear."

"Sure does. You two get the water. I want to check out this trail here—just to be sure it goes across the slide and to see how rough it is over there."

"Don't you want us to come with you?"

"No. Get the water."

"Those guys must be right next to the water. Look at that fire. It looks like there's water all the way around it. There's no island, is there?"

"No. It's just a little point of land that sticks out. I camped on it once a couple of years ago."

"I was wondering. See, those guys probably aren't too close to their motorcycles. They wouldn't take those bikes right down there on the sand. While you're over the other way, maybe I could slip around there and see if I can doctor those cycles."

"I don't know, John."

"Don't worry, Laura. I'm no hero. I won't get close to their camp. If I can zap their bikes without making any noise, I'll do it. But I won't take any chances."

"Please don't."

John put his hand on her shoulder. "You two get the water and check out that trail. I'll be back in a few minutes."

As John moved away, Amy came close and whispered, "Where's he going?"

"He's going to see if he can get close to their motorcycles."

"Shall I go with him?"

"No. I need to check out the section of trail across the slide, so I can figure how long it will take somebody to get past there. You fill up the water bottles and wait here at the junction."

"All right," Amy said. "But that's probably the worst job of all."

"I know," Laura said, slipping the pack from her back. She squeezed Amy's arm and started along the path. It was much slower going than before. The trail was not clearly established, and often there were three or four branches to choose from. Sometimes all of the forks rejoined again in a few yards, but sometimes one of them meandered for a time and simply disappeared. Given a choice of trails, Laura usually took the lower ones, even though they sometimes ended at a fishing hole.

By the time she thought to look at her watch it did no good. She had no idea whether she had been gone from Amy for five minutes or twenty. The trail was still meandering around boulders, so she was not even on the rockslide yet. The hard part still lay ahead.

She stepped over a low bush and around a boulder into a small open spot. Without knowing why, she suddenly glanced back over her shoulder into the darkness. Something had startled her—a sound perhaps. But there was nothing to see, and the only sound was that of her own breathing. As she turned forward again, a beam of light struck her eyes. She stood helplessly and stared into the blinding brightness.

XI

"Don't yell," a voice whispered. "Don't say nothing." The light clicked off, leaving Laura in what was now total darkness. Until her eyes grew accustomed to the dark again, it would be useless to try to run. And she had no idea which way to go.

"Who are you?" she asked quietly, hearing steps coming toward her.

"It's me. Myron." He stopped a few feet away from her. "How'd you get down from there?"

"It wasn't easy."

"We can sit down if you want," he said. "Just keep it real quiet." Laura squatted down where she was. In spite of everything, it felt good to let her legs relax. "I thought maybe you could get down, but old Brian was sure nobody could make it in the dark."

"It wasn't easy," Laura said again. She tried to think of something more to say—anything at all. She had to delay things until her night vision returned. "Have you and Brian been friends for a long time?" she asked finally.

"He's not really my friend. He's my stepbrother, sort of. I guess that's what you call it. My father got married to his mother last fall."

"What about Wally?"

"He lives down the road from us."

"Do you have any other brothers and sisters?" she asked, desperate for something to say.

"I got two younger sisters, but they live with my mom."

"What about Brian?"

"He's just got us. He was an only child before. You can kind of tell."

Laura understood, but she seized the opportunity. "How do you mean, Myron?"

"What's that?"

"You said you can kind of tell that Brian was an only child."

"Well, you can tell, if you know what I mean. He's used to getting his way. You know, kind of spoiled. I had a motorcycle, so he had to get one right away. Stuff like that."

"He'd be hard to live with, I'd think."

"He's all right most of the time. But you kind of have to go along with him. Otherwise, he gets all pushed out of shape."

"Like this whole business?" Laura asked gently.

"Yeah. Like this whole business."

"What are we going to do, Myron?" She could see

the outlines of the rocks and brush now. She would be ready to run if she had to.

"You just go back up there. He'll never know you came down at all."

"But we can't stay up there forever."

"I know," Myron said. "But you can't come this way. Brian sent me over here to sleep so I could keep an eye on the trail and the slide. He thought you might try to sneak somebody out in the morning."

"But he wouldn't know we came this way."

"He'd know. And he'd be on me for it."

"But this is the only way to go."

"No, it isn't. You can take this same trail the other way around the lake. It's a whole lot easier than climbing over the rocks anyway."

"But that takes us right past their camp."

"Yeah," Myron said. "You go that way, and it won't be my fault. He won't be able to blame it on me."

"But, Myron, what do you care—"

"Look," he cut in, his voice angry, "don't start on me. I gotta live with him, and you don't."

"You're right, Myron. I'm sorry."

"It's all right." He stopped for a minute. "You better go tonight. Tomorrow they're gonna come up after you. They're gonna put on their helmets and jackets and come right up after you. You got Brian real mad tonight when you were singing and all. He spent all night working on a thing to keep the rocks from hitting him. You know, like the sword fighters used to have."

"A shield?"

"Yeah, that's it. He tied branches onto that backpack he took. So tomorrow he's gonna come after you."

"What about you?"

"I don't know. I gotta live with him, see? If you're smart, you'll get your people and go on out that other way."

"All right, Myron. Thanks."

"Just don't come back this way. You go the other way, and it's not my fault. And he's not looking for you at all. He was so sure nobody could get down from there in the dark."

Laura stood up slowly. "I'll go now."

"All right. I hope you make it okay."

"Me, too."

Realizing how long she had been gone, Laura hurried back along the path, moving as rapidly as she dared. She was so intent on hurrying that she passed the trail junction without recognizing it. John reached out and caught her arm, and she had to clench her teeth to keep from screaming.

"We were getting worried," Amy said, drawing close. "You've been gone a long time."

"I thought I had the hard part," John whispered, "but I've been back here waiting for half an hour."

"How'd it go?" Laura asked.

"Like a dream. I drained the gas out of all three cycles. Mission accomplished."

"We've got to get everybody out of here tonight," Laura said. She told them briefly about her encounter with Myron.

"Those guys could never make it to the cave," John said. "We'd destroy 'em."

"I'd just as soon miss the whole thing," Laura said. "As long as you've taken care of the cycles, we all might as well get out of here together. You two go back and tell everybody to get ready."

"Where will you be?" Amy asked.

"I'll be along in a few minutes," Laura said. "I want to do some final checking." She watched them start up the trail, then turned and headed along the other path. An idea had struck her after she had left Myron, and she was still getting used to it. It frightened her, but it was the only way she could think of to stop Brian and Wally without endangering everyone.

Her plan was enormously simple: She was going to steal their shoes—if it seemed possible. She would get close enough to study the situation. Then she could decide.

As she neared the campsite, she could smell gasoline, although she couldn't spot the motorcycles. The campfire had burned low, and only an occasional flame sputtered out over the orange coals. On either side of the fire were the dark mounds of sleeping bags.

Laura left the trail reluctantly. She could follow the

established path easily, without worrying about a misstep. Once off the trail she had to feel out each move forward. The trees overhead blocked out the moon, and she could see almost nothing, even when she crouched low and tried to study the ground in front of her.

Although she moved slowly, often using her hands to feel her way, the first few yards away from the trail were simple enough. A stand of trees hid her from the sleepers. It was dark there in the shadows, but at least she was under cover. Once she reached the tree trunks, she stopped short. There was nothing between the trees and the campfire but a stretch of gravel and sand.

Was it possible? How could anybody move quietly on a gravel bar? And there was no camouflage and no place to hide. She wondered whether she could lie down on her stomach and work her way across the bar quietly enough. It seemed possible to move that way, but it would take an enormous amount of time.

She leaned against a tree and steadied herself. She did not have time to be crawling anywhere. If she spent half an hour creeping across the sandbar, there was no telling what might happen with her group. As long as she was going to take a risk, it might as well be one that made sense.

Setting her jaw, Laura took her first tentative steps on the gravel. There was the usual scrunch and scrape, but the sounds were less loud than she might have thought. She moved slowly and steadily forward, keep-

ing her eyes on the forms in front of her. Each foot-
step was as regular as she could make it. She had a
notion that perhaps it was the irregular which brought
a person out of a sound sleep—no matter how loud or
quiet the irregular happened to be.

As she continued to move forward, she suddenly
realized that a decision was upon her. She had to go
to her left or her right. Did she want to deal first with
Brian or Wally? It was the sort of decision that she
would have liked to study for a few minutes. She
forced herself to keep moving, although she was not
really deciding. All of her attention was devoted to
moving as quietly and regularly as possible. She hadn't
even realized which of the mounds was Wally and
which was Brian, although it was obvious to anyone
who looked.

She continued to move forward, deciding to circle on
the lake side and then back. It was more comforting
to think in terms of the lake side and the tree side
rather than in terms of people.

The first pair of boots were lying about three feet
from the head of the sleeper. She circled away from
the fire, still moving steadily, and brought herself
close enough in to snatch up the boots in the middle
of a stride. The sleeper, which some part of her mind
recognized as Brian, did not move.

As she circled the fire, Laura tried to locate the
other boots. Wally lay on his side, facing away from
the fire. She could hear his snoring, but it was dis-

concerting to have him facing in her direction. His boots, she finally saw, were lying next to his bag, about where his knees would be. She continued her circle, watching the huge head. As she walked, she shifted Brian's boots to her left hand. Then, stepping close to Wally, she snatched up the first boot quickly and easily. It was heavier than she expected. Before she could gather up the other, she had to shift her load. And of course, her feet were no longer moving.

The loss of rhythm frightened Laura. Her theory about regular sounds, whether or not it was correct, had given her a basis for security. Suddenly that basis was gone. She tucked Wally's boot into the crook of her arm and reached for the remaining one.

"Whaaa," Wally moaned.

Laura jumped at the sound and felt the boot slipping from her fingers. She grabbed it more tightly and felt the rest of her load begin to shift. Wally lifted an arm and rocked forward. She held onto the boots as tightly as she could, unable to move for fear of dropping one.

"Aaah," Wally moaned. He turned over slowly, the whole bag flipping with him. For a moment he was on his stomach, but he continued to roll. As he came to rest on his back, Laura felt something mash down on her foot.

Wally grumbled as he shifted slightly. His mouth dropped open, and he began to snore. His left hip rested on Laura's foot.

Laura took two long breaths and secured her grips

on the boots. Once she was certain that she wouldn't drop any of them, she tried to edge her foot out from under Wally. As she slowly drew it out, the snoring stopped. She stood rigidly, not daring to move. Wally jerked his hip, first toward her and then away. His weight was still resting on her toes. "Huh," he said. She stood and stared down at him, trying to see if his eyes were open. "Huh," he said again.

Wally shifted slightly, and his breathing became deeper and louder. Then his mouth fell open once more, and the snoring began. Laura waited as long as she could stand and then drew out her foot in one quick, steady pull. Wally gurgled once, but he continued to snore. Laura moved away quickly, trying to step with the rhythm of Wally's snoring.

When she reached the trees, she ducked behind them and set down the shoes that she had been clutching so tightly. Her fingers were cramped and stiff, and it took a minute before they were loose enough to work properly. Methodically she tied the laces together and strung both pairs of shoes around her neck. As she moved back to the path, the shoes banged together once, but the noise did not concern her. She did not think Wally and Brian would wake up, but even if they did, she sensed her advantage. How far could they chase her in their bare feet?

As the shoes grew heavier and more awkward around her neck, Laura wondered what to do with them. Her first impulse was to heave them as far into the brush as

possible, but she was afraid of the noise. Finally, tired
of carrying them, she took a few steps away from the
trail and stuffed them into the middle of a thick clump
of manzanita. Nobody would ever find them there.

She felt much freer as she hurried back to the path.

XII

Everything took longer than it should have. First the packs came down, one by one. Then Irene was lowered down, the rope tied around her waist. Then Beverly came the same way. The others climbed down the rope, but each trip took more preparation because there were fewer people left to hold the rope. Then Chris, who had held the rope alone for Stephanie, had to climb down the old way. Even with everyone's flashlight trained on the ledge, he was operating in near darkness, and he moved at a maddeningly slow pace.

Then shoes had to be restrung, and packs had to be adjusted. By the time everybody was ready to go, it was nearly four o'clock. Laura was so nervous that she was afraid to talk. She was sure that if she opened her mouth, she would scream.

The group moved slowly at first. The flashlights, which had been necessary for the final preparations, had destroyed everyone's night vision. Determined not to show a light, Laura led the way along the path,

hoping that the group's movements were not as noisy
as they seemed.

As they approached the lake and the trail junction,
the group closed ranks until they were in danger of
stepping on each other's heels. Laura moved forward,
studying the ground in front of her and trying not to
think about Brian and Wally. The campfire, now only
a reddish glow, provided no light at all.

As the odor of gasoline grew stronger, Laura kept
telling herself that nothing had changed, that Brian
and Wally would still be asleep. But she desperately
wished that she could see well enough to be certain.

Only when she had passed the motorcycles and
gotten through the sticky mud of the spilled gasoline
did she begin to relax. It was hard to believe that nine
people could move that quietly. Their steps were
painstakingly slow, of course, but now nothing lay
in front of them but the open trail.

Laura waited until they were beyond the lake before
she flipped on her flashlight. There was little chance
that anybody could see the light that far away, and it
didn't really matter anyway. The nightmare was over.
All they had ahead of them was a long walk.

Even though they were safe, they hiked at a much
faster pace than they had used before. They took an
occasional break only because Laura insisted. "We
have all day," she said, "and we got about as early a
start as anybody's ever likely to get."

When the rest of them wanted to wait until they reached Jack Pine Lake before stopping to fix breakfast, Laura had passed out cookies and agreed. At the lake Irene brought out her stove and heated water for cocoa and oatmeal. "It's still early in the morning," she said. "I figure we can spare enough time to fix something decent." Nobody argued, but as soon as breakfast was over, there was a quick move to scrub the dishes and get them repacked.

Back on the trail once more, Laura took her customary place at the end of the line. At that point the trip was simply a matter of endurance. They had eight miles ahead of them, but there was plenty of time. After the first half mile most of the trip was downhill, too. Everything considered, it was going to be a good day.

An hour went by. And then another. At each resting spot Irene and Beverly would switch off with the pack they were sharing. Each of them offered to take someone else's pack, but everyone refused. "No problem," Louie said. "Whenever I think about those ding-a-lings back there barefooted, my pack gets lighter and lighter."

When they reached the crest of the final ridge, they all cheered. Below them lay their cars, little more than a mile away. From the crest, they could see that last easy mile. The trail first crisscrossed the side of the mountain in a long series of switchbacks—all downhill. Then there was a gentler slope across open meadowland to the spot where the cars were parked.

As they sat and rested and looked down, Laura felt

a surge of warmth which she wanted to share. "Make
a circle for just a minute," she said.

The circle formed, although there was some embarrassed giggling. "It's a funny time for Ring-Around-
the-Rosy," Louie said.

"All right," Laura said once their hands were joined.
"I want to say a prayer of thanks that we're all safe
and that we're all here together. And I want you to
realize that we're all here safe because you all worked
together and stuck together. I won't force my prayer
on you. Each of you supply one of your own."

After a minute she looked up. "All right. Also, I'm
proud of all of you. Now let's put on our packs and
get down the mountain."

"We've come a long way today," John said as he
boosted his pack onto his knee. While slipping into
his pack, he glanced back at the mountains that they
had crossed. Once his pack was on, he kept staring in
that direction.

"Wrong way, klutzo," Donna said.

"Hey, Chris," John said, "come here a minute."

"What's the matter?" Amy asked. "What are you
looking at?"

"What is it?" Chris said, walking over toward John.

"Look way back," John said. "On the second ridge
back. See where that open spot is? Now, look just
below that."

"I see him," Amy moaned. "I see him."

It took Laura a minute or two to locate it—a single figure running down the trail. She watched for a moment until she was sure that there was only one person.

"Can you tell who it is?" Donna asked.

"Come on," John muttered. "From this distance?"

"I know who it is," Laura said quietly. "It has to be Brian, wearing Myron's boots."

"We ought to stay right here," Chris said. "We're uphill this time. We could make things hot for him."

"He's not worth the bother," Laura said. "We're miles ahead of him. There's no way he could catch us now."

"I'd hate to bet on it," Chris said.

"Come on," Laura said. "Let's get started. We have plenty of time to get to our cars."

There was no hesitation as they moved downward. There was enough vulnerability in the switchbacks to make them all uneasy. It was doubtful that someone could have stood at the top of the mountain and rolled rocks down onto hikers far below, but as they moved along, they kept glancing upward.

Nothing seemed to change as they came off the mountain and onto the meadowland. Somehow, Laura felt, nobody was going to feel really safe until the cars were loaded and moving down the road. Or maybe until the cars were back at home.

They had been on the meadowland about ten minutes—having covered nearly half a mile, given their pace and the terrain—when Laura heard the shout. She could not distinguish the words. It was only a shout, like the cry of an animal.

Turning back, she could see a figure standing at the top of the crest, near where they had made their circle earlier.

"I can't believe it," John said.

"Look at him," Louie said. "He came all that way just to tell us bye-bye."

Laura turned back toward the cars. "No problem. There's no way he can catch up with us now."

"But he's going to try," Chris said. "You can bet on that."

Whenever they stopped talking, they could hear the shouts. "Look at that," Louie said.

Laura turned back to the crest. "Where'd he go?"

"Can't you see him?" Louie said. "He's coming straight down."

It took Laura a moment to locate him, but then he was easy to follow. He had abandoned the trail and was plunging straight down the hill. "He's crazy," Donna said. "He's absolutely crazy."

"We'd better get moving," Chris said. "It's not going to take him long that way."

"He can't do it. There's no way he can do it," Louie said.

Laura stood and watched. From that distance he seemed too far away to pose a danger. And there was something compelling in watching the tiny human moving down the enormous mountain.

And then it happened, as somehow they all had known it would. Anyone who had hiked that mountain knew that no one could traverse it the way Brian was doing. A careful climber might have made the descent safely, but nobody could run down the face of the mountain.

Somebody screamed, although Laura could not tell who. The figure was tumbling down the mountain, falling and then bouncing and then falling again. When it finally landed, there was no more movement at all.

Laura stood for a moment, waiting to run in both directions at the same time.

"Let's go," Chris said. "We can call the Forest Service from the store at Higgins Gulch."

Laura drew in a long breath. "I hate to say it, but I think we should go back there."

"What?" Chris said. "After all he's done? Why?"

"I don't know. Because he's hurt, I guess. Because I'd feel awful if we could have helped him and didn't."

Chris shook his head. "I can't believe it."

"Look," Laura said, "I know what a rat he is, but I just can't see us going off and leaving him this way. Maybe some of you could go ahead and take one of the cars . . ."

"No," Stephanie said. Somebody else echoed her.

"I don't like this," Beverly said, beginning to cry.

"It's just . . . I don't care. If Laura is going back there, I think we all ought to go." She hesitated. "I mean, we can't run off and—"

"All right, all right," Louie cut in. "Nobody's arguing with you. But we don't have to carry our packs, do we?"

"You don't have to do this," Laura said.

"For crying out loud, Laura," Chris said, "if we're going back, let's go. He could die of old age while we're standing here arguing."

They slipped off their packs and set them beside the trail. As they retraced their steps, Laura kept watching the spot where Brian had fallen. He seemed to have moved a little, but she couldn't be sure.

They walked rapidly back across the meadow, but once they reached the switchbacks, the pace slowed. "Why couldn't he have fallen to the bottom?" Louie muttered.

"Just take it easy," Laura said as she walked past the others. "There's no use hurrying. I'm going on ahead with the first-aid kit, but please don't try to keep up."

"I'll go with you," Chris said.

Laura started to protest, then changed her mind. "That'll be great."

The two of them moved ahead steadily, resting as little as possible. Soon they were several long switchbacks ahead of the others. "Have you been keeping an eye on him?" Chris asked when they stopped to catch their breaths.

"Most of the time. It's a little hard now."

"He's not dead, at least. He's moved out of the sun, I think."

"That's good."

"I guess it is," Chris said. "When we get close . . ."

"I know," Laura told him. "I may be a little goofy, but I'm not completely crazy. I'll be careful."

Slowly they drew close. Brian lay stretched out beneath a tree, his body twisted at an odd angle. At one point, when they were on a loop directly below him, Laura wanted to call to him, but she couldn't think of anything to say. He didn't seem to be conscious anyway. So she made the last long traverse to the right and came back on the trail at his level.

Brian hadn't moved. His feet were downhill, his toes pointing skyward, but his body was bent at the waist so that he was facing the ground. He looked as if he had been lying on his back and then had turned the upper half of his body as far around as possible. The position looked tremendously uncomfortable.

Carrying the first-aid kit in her hand, Laura moved forward quickly. "Brian?" she said softly. "Brian?"

She knelt beside him, and he turned his battered face slowly toward her. There was a strange distant look in his eyes, as if he were looking through her at something that lay beyond her head. He continued to stare that way, slowly moving his left arm so that he was facing her more directly.

Only when Chris shouted "Look out!" did Laura

see the rock in Brian's right hand. The right arm, which had been lying beneath him, suddenly came to life, sending the rock directly at Laura's face. She jerked away, feeling only pain as her body pitched backward.

The rock caught her not in the face, as Brian had intended, but high on the forehead. Still, the blow knocked her off-balance, and she fell heavily on her back and slid downhill for several feet. She opened her eyes to see Chris moving past her, a huge rock in each hand.

"No, Chris!" she shouted.

"Keep your hands down," Chris shouted. "Keep 'em down, or I'll let you have it."

"Go ahead," Brian screamed. He picked up a rock and threw it upward awkwardly.

"Cut it out," Chris said, prodding Brian with his foot. "You want me to use one of these rocks on you?"

"Go ahead, you turkey," Brian screamed, pawing the ground for another rock. Chris dropped to his knees and seized both of Brian's arms. "My leg," Brian shouted, his body going limp. "It's hurt bad." Chris removed his belt and used it to lash Brian's wrists together.

"How bad is his leg?" Laura asked, climbing to her feet.

"I don't know. Right now I'm more worried about you. He got you pretty good."

Laura picked up the first-aid kit, opened it, and

looked inside. She stared for a moment at the red drops which spattered onto the white packages. Then she realized that she was the cause, that she was bleeding. "Chris," she said slowly, "I think I need some help."

"Sure, Laura." He moved close to her and took the kit from her hands. "Sit down and relax." He dabbed her forehead with antiseptic and then pushed a bandage into place. His fingers were awkward but steady. "Keep an eye on the freak," he muttered. "I'm not sure how well he's tied."

"I think he's through," Laura said.

"He sure caught you one." Chris put another piece of tape into place. "I think that'll stop the bleeding. Anyway, it should hold you till Irene gets here."

Once her forehead was bandaged, Laura looked at Brian's leg long enough to confirm that it was broken. She stepped back and sat down when she began to feel dizzy. "There's not much we can do," she told Chris. "Irene may be able to splint it or something, but we'll probably need a Forest Service stretcher crew to get him out. Too bad the whole gang had to make the trip back up here."

"No use stopping 'em now," Chris said. "They'll be here in two minutes."

"What a great bunch," Laura said.

"You kill me," Brian muttered. "Girl Scout all the way. You and your little kiddies. You make me sick." He twisted his body sideways, moaned once, and then glared at her.

Shifting her head slowly, Laura laid her throbbing head on the first-aid kit. "I'm okay," she said when Chris started toward her.

"I wish I hadn't missed you with that rock, Laura," Brian said. "I didn't want your forehead. I wanted your mouth. I wanted to send your shiny teeth down your throat. I hope I get another chance. I will, Laura. Sooner or later I'll get you. You and that turkey over there. And that old lady, too. I'll get the whole bunch of you. You'll be sorry you ever heard of me."

Laura reached into the kit and tore a strip of adhesive bandage from the spool. She drew herself to her feet, grinding her teeth at the pain, and walked slowly toward Brian.

"Hey," he shouted, "what are you doing? You stay away from me, or you'll be sorry. I mean it. You better not touch me."

Laura knelt down and fitted the wide bandage gently across his mouth. When she was sure that it was firmly in place, she stepped back and sank down.

Chris looked away from her quickly, trying to hide a grin.

"He's all right, Chris," Laura said. "He can breathe well enough through his nose."

"I wasn't worried about him. Not a bit. You try to help a guy like that, and he bashes your head in. We should never have come back. I knew it from the first."

"You're probably right."

"I can't believe you, Laura. Probably? You don't learn very fast, do you? I'll bet you'd do the same thing over again."

Laura rubbed her temples, trying to keep them from pounding so hard. "Nope. I learned something. Next time I'd look out for the rock."

As she watched her group coming up the trail toward her, Laura wondered what she *had* learned. Surely, after all she had been through, there should be something to hold onto, some bit of wisdom she had gained. *Later*, she thought. She was a different person from the one she had been three days before, but she would have to figure out the exact differences later—when her head didn't hurt so much.

Then Irene was in front of her, puffing loudly as she stripped the bandage from Laura's forehead. "Listen, honey," she said, "next time you take a notion to go camping, you leave this old lady out of it."